D1484430

LABYRINTH
OF THE
BEAST

By

Desiree Acuna

Harmony™
Erotic Fantasy Romance
New Concepts   Georgia

Be sure to check out our website for the very best in fiction at fantastic prices!

When you visit our webpage, you can:
* Read excerpts of currently available books
* View cover art of upcoming books and current releases
* Find out more about the talented artists who capture the magic of the writer's imagination on the covers
* Order books from our backlist
* Find out the latest NCP and author news--including any upcoming book signings by your favorite NCP author
* Read author bios and reviews of our books
* Get NCP submission guidelines
* And so much more!

We offer a 20% discount on all new Trade Paperback releases ordered from our website!

Be sure to visit our webpage to find the best deals in e-books and paperbacks! To find out about our new releases as soon as they are available, please be sure to sign up for our newsletter (http://www.newconceptspublishing.com/newsletter.htm) or join our reader group (http://groups.yahoo.com/group/new_concepts_pub/join)!

The newsletter is available by double opt in only and our customer information is *never* shared!

Visit our webpage at:
www.newconceptspublishing.com

New Concepts Publishing, Inc.
5202 Humphreys Rd.
Lake Park, GA 31636

ISBN 1-58608-782-7
April 2006 © Kimberly Zant
Cover art (c) copyright 2006 Jenny Dixon

NCP books are available at special quantity discounts for bulk purchases for sales promotions, premiums, fund raising, or educational use. For details, write, email, or phone New Concepts Publishing, Inc., 5202 Humphreys Rd., Lake Park, GA 31636; Ph. 229-257-0367, Fax 229-219-1097; orders@newconceptspublishing.com.

First NCP Trade Paperback Printing: June 2006

This is a work of fiction. All characters, events, and places are of the author's imagination and not to be confused with fact. Any resemblance to living persons or events is merely coincidence.

Chapter One

When Lilith woke to discover that the bear cub she'd rescued had demolished the last of the grain in her larder, she realized she could no longer put off a trek into the village. She scolded the cub, thrashing him with the brush broom and chasing him from the little shed she housed her stores in, but it did not change anything. She still had nothing to make her bread and the burst of temper did not even help her feelings, for the young bear, she knew, was only doing what came natural to him. He was hungry and so he had searched until he found something to eat. He did not understand why she was angry with him and beat the brush broom on his rump until she had broken most of the brush. She had been feeding him since she had found him alone in the forest trying to nurse his dead mother.

Panting slightly with exertion and temper, Lilith dropped the broom and glared at the cub, which had run no further than the edge of the wood and hidden beneath a frond that covered little besides the top of his head. "If you are big enough to break down my shed door then you are certainly big enough now to fend for yourself. Go back into the forest, little man. You belong there and I will not coddle you anymore!"

Instead of obeying her command, the little bear settled on the ground to watch her with mournful eyes as she turned to assess the damage and clean up the mess he had made.

There was not even enough left for a small loaf of bread, Lilith discovered, feeling her spirits plummet and anxiety begin to churn in her belly.

She hated going to the village. Everyone stared at her and whispered about her at the best of times. If she happened to arrive on the heels of someone's misfortune, instead of merely staring and whispering, they glared at her as if their misfortune was somehow her fault.

They thought she was a witch. She supposed she was, but she was no threat to them. The gifts she had could not harm anyone or bring misfortune them.

She knew that much, for she had always feared and hated the villagers, and they had always feared and hated her. There had been many times, when she had been younger and had gone to the village with her mother, that she had left the village so angry that she had tried very hard to curse them, to weave some spell that would teach them a lesson.

She did not have the power even when she had the will, and mostly, she did not have the will. She only wanted to be left alone. She had lived in the cottage her whole life, tucked safely away in the forest with her mother until the winter that had taken her mother's spirit and set it free from her body. Since that time, she had lived alone except for the animals and the trees.

She had the gift of communing with the creatures of the forest, and on occasion, she had found that she could use that same gift that soothed the wild beasts and allowed her to move among them as she pleased to bend people to her will. She knew because her mother had taught her which herbs to gather from the forest to make potions that healed, that soothed pain and fevers.

She supposed that made her a witch, but it hardly made her a creature to be feared and hated and distrusted.

There was no hope for it, though, she realized with dismay. She had no magic to make grain appear. She had no magic to make bread from dirt. She would have to go into the village and trade for grain. And if she had to go for that, she decided that she would make certain that she got all that she would need for many months so that she would not have to go again before the fall.

When she had finished cleaning up the mess the little bear

had made, she went to the well to draw water and wash the filth from her face and hands. She stared at her reflection when she had finished bathing off, wondering if it would be better to tidy herself up more, or better to go with her hair all a tangle and wear her most worn and stained dress.

She did not especially like to go into the village looking so slovenly, but she decided that it would probably be for the best. If she tried to make herself presentable and happened to catch the wandering eye of one of the village louts, they would accuse her of using witch craft to lure their men away.

As if she would have one of the pigs! she thought angrily, for there was not one, young or old, who had not tormented her when she was a child, or leered at her since she had reached womanhood and she hated the lascivious looks they gave her. She had not been with a man, but she did not need to to know what thoughts ran through their minds. They wanted to mount her and plow their man things into her body and fill her womb with their nasty seed.

She did not think that she would mind having a babe of her own, but she did not want *their* babes in her belly. One day, perhaps, she would do as her mother had and make her way to the village two days down river and find a male she was willing to couple with to have a babe, but she was in no great hurry. In any case, summer would be a better time for breeding. Then she would bear the child in the winter when there was little to do anyway and she would be strong enough to plant her garden in the spring.

Having decided that she would do as she was, she went into her yard to survey her beasts and decide which would be best to take to market for trading. Pig was huge, and ate a great deal, but he was also very good for dragging and carrying the things that were too heavy for her and he mostly foraged for his own food. She would take him, she decided, but not for trade. She would need a great many things to carry her through the season.

It would be better to trade the flock of fat geese. She was a little unhappy with the thought, for she had planned to keep them until she had enough down to make new pillows and stuff her mattress again, but it could not be helped. It would have to be the flock or the pig.

Dismissing her qualms, she went into the shed and gathered up bags for carrying her supplies, a harness for pig and her staff to herd the birds. Calling to pig when she came out, she slung the bags over his broad back and tied them securely. He was not happy about the harness, but she insisted. The villagers would be unnerved if she allowed him to roam at will, for he was a huge pig now, more than waist high to her.

When she had fashioned the harness around him, she attached a lead rope to the harness. Tucking the end into her sash, she told him to behave himself, called her flock and set out for the village, using the staff to redirect the birds whenever they would try to wander into the woods.

It was nearly noon by the time she reached the edge of the village. The geese had thoroughly exasperated her. Her shoulders were aching from swinging the staff. She was thirsty and hungry.

She supposed that was why she did not notice, at first, that an ominous quiet hung over the village. It wasn't until she glanced up and discovered the sullen glances of some of the villagers that she began to feel uneasy.

"Witch!" one of the women hissed, the comment barely audible to Lilith.

She heard, though, and more than heard for it was not as if she had not heard herself called witch before. There was a thread of hysteria in the comment that she was not used to hearing, however. Frowning, Lilith looked away at once before the woman could accuse her of giving her the evil eye.

"Look at the animals! See the way she makes them do her bidding!"

"They are so fat. Why is that she has such fat animals when all of ours are dying if it is not witch craft?" someone muttered nearby in a perfectly audible whisper.

Lilith's vague uneasiness blossomed rapidly into full fledged fear. Something had happened in the village, and they had only to set eyes upon her and she was being blamed. Realizing she'd left the pig's lead tucked into her sash, Lilith pulled it free, holding it in one hand and the staff in the other, hoping if it looked as if she was leading the beast they would not be so unnerved.

The urge to turn about and leave as she had come was strong. She saw, though, that she was already nearing the market in the center of the village before she had emerged from her contemplation of her discomfort enough to realize that the atmosphere within the village was dangerously unstable. Nursing the tiny hope that their interest in her would wane and they would go about their own business fairly quickly, she did her best to pretend to be deaf and blind to their grumbling complaints and sullen looks. The atmosphere of hate did not improve once she reached the market, however. Instead, it darkened rapidly as more and more of the villagers gathered, the growing numbers seeming to bolster the courage of those who'd first eyed her so uneasily.

The vendors, she saw in dismay, had little to sell. Most of them were gaunt, as if they had had little food for some time, and glassy eyed, as if with fever--or some madness that seemed to have gripped the entire village.

Feeling her belly tighten sickeningly, with no idea of anything else to do, Lilith tried to behave as if she had noticed nothing and headed straight for the miller, hoping to conclude her business quickly and leave. "I have geese to trade for grain," she said, keeping her voice steady with an effort.

The miller looked her over for several moments, carefully avoiding eye contact. "What about the pig?"

"He is not for trade," she said firmly. "I," she hesitated a moment. "I have trained him to carry my burdens. I will need him to carry the grain home."

He snorted. "You could carry the grain I have in a pack on your own shoulders," he growled, gesturing toward the small stack of bags behind him. "The harvest is poor this year. I do not suppose you would know ought of that?"

A wash of coldness joined the tension in Lilith's belly. Her skin grew clammy with her growing fear. "How would I know ought of that? I have not been next or nigh the village in months!"

"See! She admits it. She cursed the fields when she was here last!"

Lilith felt the hair on the base of her skull lift, realizing that the people she'd noticed gathering nearby had not come to trade as she had hoped.

She could not ignore that accusation, she realized, and glanced around to address her accuser. "I did no such thing," she said, her voice quavering slightly when she turned and discovered nearly a dozen villagers had gathered behind her. "The planting had barely begun when I was here last. Why would I have come to trade if I had known that there was nothing to trade for?"

"Came to gloat!"

"Witch!"

"Don't look in her eyes!" someone near the back of the growing crowd shouted. "She will bewitch you!"

"I only came to trade for supplies," Lilith stammered, clenching her staff a little more tightly when several of the villagers abruptly began to chase her geese about the market, trying to catch them. "What are you doing? Those are mine!"

A man jostled her, snatching the lead from her hand so that the rope left a stinging burn along her palm. The moment he did, the crowd seemed to explode into motion, as if they had only been awaiting some signal. Three men leapt at pig. Pig squealed and ran, bowling over everyone in his path. The geese squawked, running around and around in circles and flapping their wings madly. Men and women screamed, dashing around after the birds, dodging Pig, who was frightened by the people charging him and grabbing at him and only wanted to flee.

"Stop it!" Lilith cried out, her anger finally overcoming her fear enough to thaw her. "Thieves! You can not take my stock!" she yelled, beginning to lay about her with the staff. She was on the point of threatening to summon the constable when she realized that he was one of the men chasing her pig about the market place.

She had managed to beat several of the men on the back and shoulders when someone grabbed her from behind, pinning her arms to her sides. The staff was wrenched from her hands. A cloth came down over her eyes.

Screaming, she fought her captors with strength born of fear, managing to wrest free briefly before someone slammed into her back and pitched her forward into the dirt. She grunted as the air was forced from her lungs by a heavy weight.

Gritting her teeth, she wiggled and squirmed anyway, jerking against the hold on her arms as they were twisted behind her back and tied with rough hemp. The heat and stench of unwashed bodies made it evident that the crowd had gathered around her even though she could no longer see her tormentors.

"Don't let her go! Hold her!"

A mixture of terror and fury filled Lilith as they dragged her to her feet, pulling her first one way and then another, as if they were fighting over her. "Free me!" she screamed at them. "Or I *will* curse you! I will make your manhood wither and fall off!"

A gag was shoved into her mouth and bound there by something rough that bit into her cheeks before she could spit it out.

She could hear them though, bickering over what to do with her, how to make certain they rid themselves of her without risking the chance that she would be able to curse them. A wave of weakening terror washed over her and her heart began to pound so hard against her eardrums that even her sense of hearing was all but lost to her, as well.

"Take her to the cave of the beasts!" someone shouted. "Mayhap it was them who cursed us and it will appease them if we give her to them?"

"Yes!" someone else seconded the first woman. "We should take her to the beasts!"

"That is it! Give her to the evil ones! They will take her into the belly of the earth and we need not fear her curses anymore!"

Lilith would not have thought it was possible to be any more frightened than she already was, but the mention of the realm of the beasts doubled her heart rate until she thought she might pass out from sheer terror.

Her mother had told her of that place, which was not merely a great cave but a labyrinth of caves where dwelt many demons, creatures so horrific her mother could not even find the words to describe them. When her mother had been a girl, they had taken her there and left her as offering to the evil ones. She had never told Lilith what had happened to her there, only that she had escaped when few ever did. She had said that, despite what she had had to endure, she had been glad, because the 'innocent' never escaped according to the villagers. They were forgiven, having proven themselves innocent, but they did not come back. In their minds, only a powerful witch could do so, and they had been too afraid of her to bother her again when she had come back.

Lilith was in no state to appreciate that particular silver lining at the moment, however. She could think of nothing except her mother's comments that 'few survived to return to the world of man'.

She fought them, struggling with every ounce of strength she could gather to her as they lifted her off her feet and began to carry her.

Twice she almost managed to break free of them, but more hands grabbed her, pulling at her, binding her more tightly still.

They began almost to chant as they bore her off to the labyrinth. "Vanquish the witch! Our crops will flourish and our children will not go hungry!"

* * * *

Lilith had expended her strength long before they reached the place where the evil ones dwelt. The vague hope that her weakness would make them feel less threatened was quickly extinguished, however. When they had set her on her feet at last, they held her up and tore the bindings from her. Her clothing, already in tatters from their attack, was ripped from her, as well, until she stood shivering, feeling the chill of the air on her skin. Her flesh crept from the lascivious gazes of the villagers, but she could not wrest her hands free to cover herself.

"She is without flaw! Look! Her skin is as smooth as cream! She is one of them, else she would not look so perfect!" a woman said, hysteria in her voice.

"Her skin is as milky white and smooth as alabaster and the hair on her woman's mound bright as fire--to tempt men and fire their minds to madness!"

A mixture on anger and despair filled Lilith, for she knew very well that if she had been pock marked, or covered in warts and moles they would have seen those as the kiss of the demons and called her a witch regardless.

"If that is true, then perhaps they will not want her back. What will we do then?"

"Burn her!"

"Let us hide at the ridge and watch. If they do not come for her, we can gather brush and burn her!"

Lilith shuddered, summoning the strength to fight them

again as she felt the bindings loosen on her wrists. Despite the fact that she fought them with the desperation born of the desire to survive, the battle was short lived. She had fought her captors most of the way from the village and she had little reserve.

She was shoved against a hard surface that bit into the tender flesh of her back. Grabbing her arms, someone--two men--tugged, pulling them out to her sides despite her efforts to resist. She heard the clink of chains and something cold and hard closed around her wrists. A moment later, her ankles were seized in the same manner and her legs pulled from beneath her. She gasped as her weight settled on her shoulders, almost wrenching them from the sockets. She found though, once they had locked the manacles around her ankles that she could touch the ground with the soles of her feet, supporting enough weight off of her arms to ease the strain.

Her heart was pounding painfully in her chest when they stepped away from her at last. For many moments she could do nothing but focus on that, trying to calm the frantic pace, trying to fight back the nausea of fear before she choked on her own bile.

After a few minutes, she realized she could hear their retreat across the stone, the scattering of tiny pebbles and rocks.

Silence descended. She tugged at the manacles uselessly, only succeeding in draining more strength she could not afford to lose. Time passed. She had no idea of how much time, for her fear made the seconds seem agonizingly long. After a while, though, slowly but surely, discomfort began to usurp her fear. As her fear began to subside, she struggled to think of some way she might save herself, of something that she could do. After trying several times to peer beneath the binding over her eyes she began to try to rub her head against the rock behind her to dislodge it.

A sound nearby made her freeze. She listened intently,

struggling to hear over the frantic pounding of her heart. Abruptly, she identified the sound she heard as the flapping of wings, huge wings. Renewed fear squeezed at her heart. A bird of prey? Tipping her head, she tried again to peer beneath the blindfold. She could see nothing at first, but abruptly something huge and dark landed directly in front of her.

Her flesh pebbled all over her body, trying to lift the fine hair on her nape. Coldness washed over her as the creature folded its wings and moved toward her.

It looked very much like a man, but she knew it wasn't.

Its wings were those of a great, golden condor.

Its skin was dark, the color of teak.

It was a black demon, she realized abruptly, for his eyes were the same golden yellow as his wings.

She jumped all over when he lifted a hand and smoothed it down her body, as if testing the texture of her skin. Apparently not satisfied until he had examined her skin all over, he continued to stroke his hands over her belly, squeezed her breasts experimentally and then stroked his hands over her arms. She tried not to think how much his actions reminded her of testing meat for tenderness at the market.

Finally, he knelt in front of her. Lifting his hands, he placed his thumbs along the full lips of her sex and parted them. Lilith was too stunned to move or even to consider trying to evade his touch, but she flinched all over instinctively at his touch.

Paralyzed by horror, she peered down at him as he leaned toward her. A jolt went through her as she felt the heat of his breath, and then the hot, moist heat of his mouth as he opened it over her sex, sending another hard shock wave of fear through her. Every muscle in her body seemed to clench with the expectation of feeling the painful slice of his teeth. Instead, to her stunned surprise, she felt his tongue lap against her several times, almost experimentally.

She gasped at the strange, quivery sensation that washed through her. Her belly clenched convulsively.

Apparently pleased with the taste of her flesh, he settled closer, began to lick at her almost hungrily. After a moment, he pulled a tiny nub of flesh into his mouth and sucked on it.

She bucked then, trying to escape the heated lathe of his tongue. He grabbed her hips, holding her still, and continued to lap and suckle at her hungrily until a strange heaviness settled over her. Her head began to spin as if she'd drunk too much wine.

Almost as abruptly as he'd knelt to taste her, he stopped, rising to his full height. "They will be pleased with the offering," he murmured, his voice deep, husky, sending quivers through Lilith.

Her mind was so chaotic that it took her several moments to realize what he meant by the comment. She didn't know whether to be relieved or more terrified when understanding dawned. Being burned alive held no appeal, however, and she tried to convince herself that whatever else the demons had in mind for her, it could not be harder to endure than being burned alive.

A tug at her ankles distracted her from her mental chant to try to calm herself, and she peered beneath the blindfold to see that he was unfastening the manacles.

It was impulse that inspired her to try to kick him, and a poor one at that.

He caught her legs without any apparent effort, but she could see she'd angered him only by attempting to fight him. He leaned down until his mouth was near her ear. "You will not survive this, little bird, if you fight, for you will only excite them and inspire them to tame you. And that is far worse than merely entertaining themselves with you."

Lilith swallowed with an effort as he straightened away from her and turned to release the manacles on her wrists.

She didn't try to fight him again. As frightened as she was, she had her wits about her now. Even if she succeeded in escaping him, she realized, the villagers were waiting on the ridge. They would capture her, and either return her to the demon, or they would burn her at the stake.

She was alive. As long as there was breath in her body, there was a chance to survive.

He scooped her off her feet when he'd freed her. "Put your arms around my neck, little bird, for you have no wings to fly."

She was still trying to decide whether to obey his command or ignore it when she felt her belly drop in a freefall as he leapt upward and the sound of rushing air and flapping wings filled her ears. She clutched at his neck tightly then, burrowing her face against his neck fearfully.

Chapter Two

It seemed to Lilith that they soared through the air for an endless time, but she knew her fear probably only stretched time, for it could not have been long. Her belly told her when they began to descend, executing another freefall. She felt the cessation of movement briefly as he settled to the earth, and then the gentle jolts as he carried her on foot for a time.

Finally, he set her upon her feet. She wavered, but caught herself as he moved around behind her. The binding holding the gag in place was tugged free, plucking hairs from her scalp painfully. Ignoring the stinging pain, she spat the gag out gratefully, trying to gather moisture into her mouth again.

The blindfold followed the other binding.

She was almost sorry for the lack of it when the creature moved around in front of her again for she'd had no more than a brief glimpse of him before.

He was huge, towering over her and impossibly broad across his shoulders.

His body, she saw, although shaped very much like a mortal man, differed almost as drastically as it was similar, for there seemed to be no part of his body that did not bulge with hard, glistening flesh or long, ropy muscles. He was hairless. She could not see anything more than fine down on any part of him.

And she saw all of him, for he was as naked as she was-- more naked. Hair formed a veil over her woman's place. His man root had no hair any where around it to disguise the enormity of it. Flaccid, it hung more than halfway down his long thigh and was as big around as her forearm.

Unable to tear her gaze from the massive bludgeon, she closed her eyes.

He hooked a fist beneath her chin and pushed her face up. "By what name are you called, little bird?" he asked in the deep voice that had sent shivers through her before.

She opened her eyes to look up at him. His features were sharp, angular, but not unpleasing to the eye--in fact, they were strangely beautiful in an exotic way. "Lilith," she said with an effort.

"I am called Gaelen," he murmured, his golden eyes narrowing as he examined her face. Something flickered in his eyes as he examined her face slowly a second time. An arrested expression settled over his sharp features, almost of recognition. "I am a Hawkin, guardian of the gateway into the labyrinth. I serve those who dwell here," he said slowly after a tense moment had passed.

Lilith couldn't prevent a shiver from scraping down her spine anymore than she could prevent horrific images from flickering through her mind.

His gaze met hers almost as if he knew the frightened thoughts skittering through her mind. "It is my duty to protect you and to prepare you for them."

Confusion flickered through her and a tiny spark of hope. "I do not think I understand."

He tilted his head. "You are a mortal." Removing his hand from her chin, he lifted her arms, examining her wrists. "You are frail, even for a mortal, but I sense strength in you and wisdom. They are not always careful with their playthings. That is why I am to protect you. To see that you survive so that they may all have a taste of you."

He released her arms and caught her chin again, his gaze stern now. "But beware. If they think you are too frail, they will not be pleased and they will simply dispatch you.

"You are marred by the handling of yon mob," he added, almost contemptuously. "Come, I will soothe your hurts.

The horde is accustomed to only the most beautiful mortals. They will not be pleased to see you as you are now."

Bewildered, but oddly soothed by his assertion that he would care for her and the gentleness he had displayed toward her thus far, Lilith allowed him to take her hand and lead her.

They were in a natural corridor, she saw, lit here and there by flickering torches. The rocky tunnel descended ever so slightly, she realized fairly quickly, feeling the pull in her muscles. After walking for perhaps ten minutes, they emerged into a wider space that created a room of sorts. It was used for that purpose, she saw, for there were furnishings in it--a narrow bed, a table and chair. A brazier stood in the center, warmth radiating outward from the smoldering coals it contained. Smoke crawled along the low ceiling and out of 'doorway', drifting along the ceiling of the tunnel they had just traversed.

"If you have need to relieve yourself, you may go there," he said, pointing to a narrow opening along another wall of the 'room'.

She thought she did, but she was so frightened she wasn't certain if it was bodily need or merely the fear. Nodding, she moved away when he released her and crossed to the narrow opening. She saw when she looked inside, that it was a small chamber much like the one she'd just left. When she'd quickly taken care of her needs, she returned the way she'd come since there was no alternative.

The Hawkin was crouched before the brazier, carefully settling a skewered hare over the coals. Her stomach immediately clenched in demand. She licked her lips, realizing that in spite of everything, she *was* hungry.

He looked up when she returned and straightened. "Come. I will bathe you and then salve your hurts and then you may eat."

Trying to staunch the dread that immediately assailed her, Lilith didn't resist as he took her hand and led her through another opening. The sound of trickling water assailed her almost at once and her throat closed.

"There is water there to appease your thirst."

Lilith glanced at Gaelen and then followed the direction of his pointing finger.

Water trickled from the rock of one wall and into a small, natural basin. Hurrying to it the moment he released her, she scooped up handfuls of water and drank greedily until the cold water had numbed her hands and a painful throbbing began in her head.

"Enough," he murmured, catching her arm and leading her away from the water. She resisted when she saw that he was leading her to a pool in the floor of the cave. He either didn't notice, or he simply ignored her effort to resist.

She stared fearfully at the frothing, bubbling water. "It will boil my flesh from my bones."

"Nay. It is not as hot as that," he disagreed, pointing to a flat rock just below the water's edge. "Sit there."

Gingerly, Lilith poked her toe into the water. Discovering that he hadn't lied to her--for the water was hot, but not uncomfortably so--she settled as she'd been told, drawing into a tight, self protective knot and glancing around the chamber uneasily. Grabbing up a cake of soap and a cloth that lay beside it, he waded into the pool, lathering the cloth liberally. She jumped when he grabbed her ankle, but at the warning look he sent her, the fight went out of her if not the uneasiness. She sat perfectly still as he rubbed the cloth over her feet and legs. When he was satisfied, he took her arms and repeated the process and then began to lather her body. Uncomfortable as she was with his familiarity, a curious warmth began to gather inside of her as he stroked her with the cloth. Feeling strangely awkward, she searched her mind for something to distract her mind from what he was doing. "Why did you … do that to me when you found me at the rock?"

His gaze flickered to her face. His eyes seemed almost to

glow with heat. "To make certain that you were tender and sweet."

Lilith blinked rapidly at that, feeling her heart seize in her chest. She swallowed with an effort. "They will eat me?" she asked fearfully.

His gaze sharpened, a frown appearing between his brows. Abruptly, he chuckled.

The sound made her belly clench, but, oddly enough, it was not altogether from nerves for it was a strangely pleasant sound.

"You would not make many bites for them, little bird. They will be far more interested in playing with you," he said almost gently.

Lilith swallowed with an effort. As assurances went, she didn't feel terribly relieved. A tangle of images instantly flickered through her mind, but although she was absolutely certain from the heated look he gave her that the 'play' he spoke of was sexual in nature, her mind simply refused to produce images of anything she could consider 'play', for the only intercourse between two creatures that she'd ever observed was the brief coupling between her animals.

He distracted her from her anxiety, however, by grasping her ankles and pulling her legs apart. Embarrassed, Lilith resisted. He merely exerted more strength, shoving her knees up and settling them on either side of her hips. "Do not move," he growled, his voice threatening now.

Swallowing with an effort, resisting the urge to leap to her feet and run, Lilith squeezed her eyes closed and held as still as she could while he took the soapy cloth and bathed her cleft with a thoroughness that left her gasping.

When he was finally satisfied, he grasped her waist and dragged her into the pool, holding her against him and using one hand to rinse the lather from her. His man root bumped her thigh, hardened, slipped between her legs. Her eyes widened as she felt it bump against her cleft.

He sent her a smoldering glance, but he made no attempt to either remove it, or to do anything more. Instead, he settled her feet until she was touching the bottom of the pool and washed her hair as he had her body.

When he had rinsed the soap from her hair, he lifted her onto the ledge again, released her and climbed out of the pool. Unable to resist, Lilith stared at his man root as he emerged, feeling her throat close when she saw that it was even bigger than before, standing away from his body now.

Moving behind her, he leaned down and wrapped his enormous hands around her, just beneath her breasts, lifting her to her feet. She glanced at his face a little fearfully, but he released her as soon as she was standing, wrapped his fingers around her upper arm and led her back to the bed chamber. Leaving her near the brazier to dry in the heat, he squatted down in one corner to examine something in a chest he'd opened. After a moment, he turned his head, studied her for several moments and finally closed the chest again and rose to his full height, tucking the small chest he'd lifted beneath one arm.

Lilith tensed as he approached her, but she knew it was useless to attempt to struggle. Besides, he had told her that fighting would get her killed, she reminded herself. The only hope she saw of surviving was to try to cooperate.

She hoped that would ensure her survival, anyway.

It certainly did not take any great intelligence to realize that fighting would avail her nothing more than a swift end, for this demon was easily twice her size and only one of many, and he would need no help to tear her to shreds if the notion struck him.

Grasping her arm again, he led her to the bed and turned her to face him. As she watched, he set the small chest beside the bed and flipped it open again, taking something from it. She saw when he straightened that it was a large metal ring, darkened with age. Around the circumference of it, loops of metal had been fastened. He pulled on the ring and to her surprise it opened. Pushing her hair out of the way, he encircled her neck with the thing and closed it again with a tiny latch.

Feeling more puzzled than threatened, Lilith lifted a hand to explore the ring with her fingers as he pushed her down until she was seated on the edge of the bed.

Pushing her back, he grasped one of her arms and drew it out to her side. Lilith's eyes widened when she saw the manacle he dragged up from the headboard. "What are you doing?" she gasped in suddenly renewed fear.

"Making certain you are not hurt," he said calmly, fastening the manacle tightly around her wrist. "I can not chance that you will not try to struggle and then you would be injured."

She did struggle. She fought him with blind panic as he very calmly grabbed her other wrist and manacled her free arm to the other end of the bed. When he'd locked the manacle around her wrist and straightened, she lay panting, watching him fearfully as he grabbed her leg, bent her knee until her foot was resting on the bed and then took another manacle and secured it around her ankle. He caught her other leg and repeated the process despite the brief battle that ensued when she tried to jerk her foot from his grip and kick him.

Cool air caressed her sex as the tightening manacle spread her legs so wide it pulled painfully at the tendons between her thighs and the petals of flesh that usually protected her sex parted, exposing the more tender flesh beneath.

Thoroughly frightened by now, but unable to move, Lilith watched him with wide frightened eyes as he bent to the chest again. Lifting it up, he settled it on the bed beside her and then pulled a jar from it. Dabbing his fingers into some sort of creamy substance, he smeared a dollop on each of her nipples and then knelt beside the bed and pushed the flesh of her sex wider and dabbed more there.

He hesitated a moment and then slipped his hand down to

the opening of her body, pushing a finger slowly inside of her. Lilith's breath caught in her chest. Frantically, she pulled at the manacles, trying to move away from his exploration, only to discover she couldn't move more than a fraction of an inch in any direction other than toward him. Ignoring her frightened thrashing, frowning in concentration, he moved his finger around inside of her.

Apparently, he found what he'd expected to find, for he grunted, slowly withdrew his finger and got to his feet. Leaning down he plucked at her nipples until they were hard and erect. It was only then that Lilith realized the cream he had dabbed on her skin had numbed her flesh to sensation. She felt the tugging, but little beyond that.

Some of her fear abated with the realization that he could not mean to cause her pain if he had taken the time to dull sensation. She was still anxious, wondering what he meant by it, but she did not have many moments to worry over it, for he lifted a thin length of chain from the trunk and dropped it onto her belly. When his hand emerged from the trunk again, she saw he was holding several shiny rings, tiny rings little bigger than the links of the chain he'd placed on her belly.

Leaning over her again, he took one nipple between his fingers, pinched it tightly at the base and pushed one of the rings through the tip. Realizing what he was about to do moments before, Lilith squeezed her eyes closed, but she felt little more than an uncomfortable tug and a mild stinging. She still tensed as he grabbed her other nipple and repeated the process.

Relieved when the tugging stopped, she opened her eyes again, watching as he threaded the thin chain through one of the loops and attached one end to the collar around her neck.

Straightening the chain, he moved down, kneeling at the edge of the bed again and grasping a tiny bud of flesh at the apex of her thighs. When he'd pinched it as he had her nipples, he pushed the remaining ring through the flesh, threaded the chain through it and then upward through her other nipple ring, attaching it to the other side of the collar around her neck.

She'd almost drawn a breath of relief when he dipped his fingers into the jar again. Tensing instinctively, she felt almost as if someone had jerked a rug out from under her when, instead of dabbing the cream on her, he caught his cock in one hand and began to slather the cream on his member, massaging it into his skin.

As she watched, the flesh hardened.

Even when he knelt on the floor she didn't realize his intention until she felt his fingers spreading her flesh, felt the hard knob at the end of his cock as he pressed it against her. Numbed as she was, she could still feel her flesh resist at the enormity of his member as he caught her hips and pushed. Slowly, steadily, he pushed, embedding his flesh deeper and deeper inside of her. Something deep inside her seemed almost to pop, giving way beneath his insistent pressure. She gasped, feeling a radiant heat wash through her, twinges of pain that the numbing cream didn't completely obliterate.

When he'd pushed into her until he could go no deeper, he began to pull away. Relief flooded her. It was short lived. He'd no more than pulled back before he began to push into her again, slowly, like before. Her belly clenched, resisting, but his thrust was relentless. Again he pushed into her until he could go no deeper and again, after a brief pause, withdrew.

Each time that he withdrew until only the head of his cock remained inside of her, she thought that he would stop. He didn't. He continued to thrust and pull back over and over. The numbness began to wear off after several minutes. Her nipples began to throb as did the nub of flesh between her thighs that he'd pierced. Inside her passage, she became more and more aware of the stroking movements as he continued to pump his thick flesh into her passage.

She tried to relax, tried to close her mind to the intrusion but found it impossible. His man root was enormous, hard, and his flesh stretched hers almost to the point of pain.

As the feeling returned, his did also. Tiny beads of sweat began to glisten on his body as he continued his slow pumping into her and out of her passage. He gritted his teeth. Almost as if it was against his will, he began to move faster until he was thrusting into her in hard jolts that tugged at her bindings.

Heat began to blossom in her belly, an odd tension and expectancy washing over her. It built, growing stronger and stronger. The sensation was strangely pleasant and grew more and more intensely enjoyable until she found she could not be still. She began to writhe, feeling fevered, dizzy as the sensations grew more pronounced. Soft moans seemed wrenched from her chest. Abruptly, the building tension seemed to explode outward in a hail of fiery rapture that made her body tingle all over. It wrenched a cry from her.

He shuddered as she cried out. Uttering a hoarse groan, he pounded into her harder and harder until he went still abruptly, jerking and shaking. Something hot spilled inside of her as he stopped, his fingers digging into her flesh, his breath hoarse and gasping.

With an effort, she opened her eyes a slit as she felt his flesh withdrawn at last from her body. Breathing heavily, he got to his feet and turned away. Limp, and unable to move even if she'd had any strength at all in her limbs, Lilith closed her eyes again.

She opened them when she felt the mattress dip beneath his weight.

"It will be easier next time," he murmured, settling a platter of food on her belly. Grabbing a pillow, he lifted her head and pushed the pillow beneath it.

Still feeling strangely lethargic, Lilith merely stared at

him in surprise when he pulled a small piece of rabbit from the tray and touched it to her lips. "Eat," he commanded. "You will need your strength."

She would have far preferred feeding herself, but she found that she was very hungry as she chewed the bite of meat and swallowed. As difficult as it was to eat lying down, he obviously didn't intend to release her any time soon.

Her belly clenched when she realized what that meant.

Trying to dismiss the thought, she focused on eating. Tearing off small bits of food, he would give her a bite and then take a morsel for himself. After a few moments, when she'd begun to think she would choke from the lack of moisture in her mouth, he fed her a grape. The plump fruit burst in her mouth, filling it with sweet juice.

"Why were your eyes covered?"

Lilith glanced at him in surprise. "They were afraid that I would bespell them with my gaze."

His brows lifted. "And the gag?"

"So that I could not curse them."

Amusement gleamed in his eyes. "They believe you are a witch?"

"Yes."

His gaze flickered over her, lighting on the nest of curling hair on her mound. As if he could not resist, he lifted a hand and explored it with his fingers. "But they did not touch you. You are fearsome for a little bird."

Lilith frowned in confusion. "They bound me and brought me here."

He tore off another bite of hare, bit down on it, tearing a piece off, and then fed the remainder to her. "You were a maiden."

Was, but she didn't need him to tell her she wasn't any more. Her passage still throbbed from his possession. "Why did you do that?" she asked, trying to keep her voice from quivering.

He tilted his head to study her face. After a moment, he frowned. "I did not give you pain. I was very careful."

Relatively little--very little considering the size of him, she supposed, knowing it could have been far worse. "But … I did not fight."

His lips curled at the lie. "Your fight was not effective. You have fire in you. Take care or they will quench it."

Lilith swallowed audibly.

He plucked another grape and touched it to her lips. When she'd swallowed it, she sent him a reproachful glance. "You said you were here to protect me. I have--tried very hard to do just as you bade me."

He studied her frowningly for several moments and finally shrugged. "I took your maiden head because I was willing to be gentle and cause you little pain. If I had left it, you would have felt much pain when they took it. Your body has not known a man, but it will grow accustomed. This will make it easier for you."

Lilith wasn't sure whether she believed that or not--or the intention he claimed. He had called himself a Hawkin, but she knew that was only a word for his particular kind. He was a demon, just as the others were that dwelt within the labyrinth and they were notoriously bad about lying.

"And because I wanted it for myself," he added pensively.

Surprised, Lilith met his gaze. "Why?"

Several emotions seemed to flicker across his face. "I felt … a hunger," he responded finally, slowly, as if he wasn't entirely certain of the answer. His gaze moved over her thoughtfully. "A need?" he said questioningly, as if he was testing the word. A faint smile curled his lips. "Mayhap you bespelled me?"

"I do no know how to cast spells. If I did, I would not be here."

He frowned as he picked up the last grape. After studying it a moment, he gave it to her and then lifted the tray from her stomach and set it aside.

Lilith watched him warily as he rose from the bed, her belly clenching when he knelt as he had before, dipped his hand into the jar and began to stroke it over his member until it was engorged.

Swallowing with an effort, she cast around desperately for something to distract him. "Why do you do that? You can not ... feel pleasure, can you?"

He looked up at her. "I can, but not so much that I can not hold my seed. In this way, I can have more pleasure ... and give you pleasure."

Holding her gaze, he aligned the head of his cock with her body and began to push.

Her eyes widened as she felt the resistance of her body to his possession. She gasped, panted for breath as he slowly pushed deeper. His eyelids slid half closed, but he watched her face, pulling away slightly when the resistance of the muscles along her passage reached the point of pain and then pushing again. The moisture of the cream and his seed from before mingled, easing his path after a moment until, despite the tightness, he'd buried himself deeply inside of her.

He paused then. Opening her eyes to see why, she discovered that he was looking down at the juncture of their bodies, his face twisted almost as if he was in agony. Lifting one hand, he flicked at the ring in the bud at the top of her cleft. Vibrations of sensation rippled through her, such pleasurable sensation that Lilith gasped again. The faint sound drew his gaze like a magnet.

Watching her face once more, he withdrew until only the head of his cock was inside of her and thrust deeply again, teasing the keenly sensitive bud with his finger. Lilith's belly clenched around his flesh, heat and excitement building in her and pumping through her blood. The weak lethargy from before swept through her as she watched the glide of his dark flesh into her passage and then out again. Within moments, she felt as if she was on fire, found she could no longer hold her eyes open or be still. Tremors wracked her. Her hips lifted fractionally, seemingly of their own volition as he impaled her again to the hilt of his man root once more.

As if the movement had ignited him, he let out a harsh breath and began to move faster, driving deeply inside of her each time and withdrawing from her more and more quickly. She gasped, groaning as the heat wave inside of her built until she knew what was coming, an explosion of ecstasy. She cried out with the force of it as it began to rock through her.

He echoed her cry with a harsh groan, thrusting into her almost frenziedly for several moments before he, too, began to quake with release.

Lilith was so drained with the second rush that she went perfectly limp when the echoes began to die away, drifting toward the edge of consciousness and then falling over the edge.

She roused slightly when she felt a tug on her wrists and then her ankles, groaning at the pain of strained muscles as he removed the manacles, shifted her around on the bed and then, to her surprise, left her in peace.

Chapter Three

When Lilith woke, she thought for several moments that she was in her own bed, in her own little cottage in the forest. As her mind drifted over the 'dreams', though, she frowned, trying to decide what would make her dream such a thing. She realized after a few moments that it hadn't been dreams at all and opened her eyes.

Gaelen was seated at the other end of the bed, watching her broodingly. He looked away when he saw she was studying him. When he glanced at her again, he jerked his head toward the room where she'd relieved herself before.

Realizing she had the need, she stumbled out of the bed and went, wondering sluggishly how long she'd slept. It didn't seem to her that it could possibly have been long, but it had been long enough, she quickly discovered, for her muscles to complain painfully over the things that she'd been through the day before.

He met her at the opening when she came out, leading her to the pool where she'd bathed before. Without a word, he guided her to the flat rock and bathed her. She bit her lip as he rubbed the soapy cloth over her skin. His hand stilled. "What is this?" he demanded, flicking a finger over the frown between her brows.

"My body hurts from … from…."

The displeasure vanished from his eyes. He finished bathing her, but more gently. Despite that, Lilith's belly clenched with nerves as he led her back to the room and pushed her toward the brazier to warm herself and dry off.

"Come," he said after a few moments.

When Lilith turned, her heart seemed to flip over, for she could see he'd just taken something from the chest. She settled nervously on the edge of the bed. To her surprise, he made her lay down on her belly. The scent of oil filled her nostrils. A moment later, his big hands settled on her. Despite her best efforts, she flinched, tensing all over.

His hands, covered in the oil, moved over her back and shoulders in a motion that soothed, though. The muscles complained, but even the pain seemed oddly pleasurable and as he moved over her, kneading her flesh, the pain began to subside. She was more than half asleep when he finally ceased to rub her.

She didn't even consider objecting when he told her to roll over onto her back. She discovered the moment he began to rub her breasts, though, that the massaging motion of his hands had the opposite effect as they had had before. Warmth blossomed in her belly. Tingles of exquisite sensation radiated outward and collected in her woman's place as his palms teased her nipples. By the time he'd moved down to her belly, she was having trouble regulating her breathing, and great difficulty remaining still.

Lifting her legs and bending her knees, he settled at the foot of the bed and lifted one leg, rubbing it as he had her back in firm stroking motions. Her belly began to clench and unclench spasmodically as he massaged her thigh and finally settled her foot and lifted the other leg.

She saw when she finally nerved herself to look down at him that his gaze was fixed on the bright, curling thatch of hair between her legs. His expression was taut. His eyes, shuttered by half closed lids, seemed to glow with an internal fire.

She closed her eyes, trying not to think about his fascination with her sex.

Her eyes popped open again when he dropped her foot to the mattress and caught her hips, lifting them from the bed. Before she could even gasp, he had covered her mound with his mouth. Her body seemed to seize as his heat invaded her. He sucked the bud of flesh, teasing the ring with his tongue and sending hard jolts of pleasure through her. She gasped, bucked against the remorseless assault on her senses. His hands tightened possessively. Hungrily, he licked and sucked at her tender flesh until she began to feel the burgeoning of heat within her belly again. She gasped raggedly, trying to catch her breath, her mind and body on fire.

A ragged cry was torn from her as her body crested, convulsed in merciless spasms as he continued to feed on her flesh until she was screaming and the pleasure had begun to skate the edge of pure torment.

Relief washed over her when he finally lifted his head. Her body trembled, jerked, still throbbing and pulsing as he lowered her to the mattress. For many moments, she could do nothing but fight the blackness crowding her mind, struggling to drag air into her lungs. She was as limp as a rag doll when he slipped his arms around her and pulled her upright. Pulling her onto his lap, he settled her legs on either side of his thighs and caught her against his chest. She dropped her forehead against his hard shoulder weakly.

"Mount me," he whispered huskily against her ear.

Still dazed, Lilith wobbled as she tried to comply and finally merely offered no resistance as he guided her with his hands, lifting her up onto her knees and guiding his engorged member into the mouth of her passage. She caught her breath as he began to bear down on her, looping her arms weakly around his shoulders to keep her balance, biting her lip as the pressure became more and more intense until she was certain she could not take him more deeply, and still he pushed inexorably, lifting his hips and grinding into her until she whimpered, fearing he would split her two.

He stopped, his breath as ragged as hers. After a moment, he began to stroke her back almost soothingly. The pain subsided. Some of the pressure of his flesh pushing against hers eased. He slipped a hand around her, flicking at the ring in her bud. The moment he did so, pleasure washed through her and her body tightened around his flesh.

He uttered a pained grunt and grabbed her hips, lifting her up and driving her down onto his shaft again and again. With each movement, her nipples dragged along his chest, the rings sending sharp jolts through her until she was moaning incessantly. Rapture ruptured inside of her violently, explosively, tearing a keening cry from her. As if the sound had sent him beyond return, Gaelen found his own release, grinding her down against his body and tightening his arms around her as it quaked through him until she began to think he would crush her.

Almost as if he heard her distress, his arms loosened abruptly. Tremors were still shaking his body as he caught her hips, tipped her over onto her back and settled weakly on top of her.

They lay entangled so long that Lilith drifted off to sleep again. She woke when he lifted away from her and left the bed. Realizing after a few moments that he had left the room, as well, Lilith sat up, trying to shake the lethargy that still lingered.

She sat where she was for a time, uncertain of whether she would arouse his wrath or not if he returned and found her gone. The stickiness of his seed discomfited her, though, and finally she crept from the bed and went down to the pool to bathe off.

Gaelen stepped through the 'corridor' doorway as she returned. He studied her frowningly for several moments but finally merely jerked his head toward the bed. He had food, Lilith saw, and he had only just pleasured himself with her. Certain she had nothing to be anxious about, she moved to the bed, settling at one end.

He settled beside her, set the tray down and pulled her onto his lap. Snuggling her against his shoulder, he plucked food from the tray, handing her a small bunch of grapes before grabbing some for himself. Too weak and weary to do anything but relax, Lilith didn't even try to remain aloof.

"You are not afraid of me," he said after a few moments in his deep, rumbling voice, sounding surprised.

Lilith glanced at his face. "I am. I am terrified."

His gaze met hers. "You were afraid that I would hurt you. 'Tis not the same. You are a strange mortal."

Lilith grimaced. She had heard that before. It was her strangeness that kept her alone, for people distrusted and feared, or hated, anyone who was different. She supposed, in a way, he was right about her fear, or lack of it. She discovered she *was* afraid, but not terrified as she probably should be. She wondered if that was because she was more accustomed to the behavior of animals than people. Animals were never cruel. They killed when they were hungry and they attacked only when they were frightened or hurt. They didn't kill, or torture, or maim for pleasure and because she understood them, she wasn't afraid of them, knew when she was safe around them and when she was not.

"We are all beasts," he said, sounding displeased. "Even humans."

Lilith glanced at him in surprise, but there was only one conclusion to draw from his comment. "You hear my thoughts?"

"When I want to know them."

That disconcerted her for she doubted that it was possible to guard one's mind from dangerous thoughts.

"Your thoughts--interest me. Do I please you? Is that why you do not look at me in fear?"

Lilith felt a blush rise to heat her face.

He chuckled, tipping her face up to study it. "I did not mean that, little bird. I watch your face when I join my body with yours, hear the sounds of your pleasure. I know that I can satisfy you in that way. I mean, is my form pleasing to you when you have not seen the like of such as me before? My appearance did not seem to frighten you and yet most mortals who look upon me cringe in fear."

She studied his face, realizing she did find it pleasing. "That is because of what you are, not because your appearance is dreadful. Why do you call me little bird?"

He looked surprised. She wasn't certain if it was the question or the fact that she had readily admitted that his appearance was pleasing to her, but she had seen no sense in trying to lie when he read her thoughts so easily.

He shrugged. "It came into my mind when I saw you." He lifted one of her hands, examining it. Releasing it, he brushed a hand along her belly. "Your flesh is pale as milk, your hair as brilliant as fire. Your eyes are bright with intelligence and curiosity and your body tiny and frail.

"Tell me about your little cottage in the deep woods and the beasts who come to you when they are hurt."

She was surprised that he seemed interested in knowing, and wondered if he had only urged her to talk because he was trying to lull her fears. She had been content enough with her life, happy, as often as not, but she could not think it would be all that interesting to anyone.

She told him, though, about what she did with the endless progression of days.

She found it oddly soothing to talk about her life before. It was better than thinking about what had happened in the village, and far better than dwelling on what would happen to her now.

She didn't delude herself into thinking that what she had experienced was even near the worst of it. He had said he was there to make certain that she survived and she didn't want to think of what she would have to endure if she needed his tender care to do so.

He fed her tidbits of food, sometimes placing it in her hand, at others into her mouth--as if she was a bird, a pet to be stroked and petted, for he did that, too, stroked her skin as if he found pleasure in running his hands along it to feel her softness.

When she could think of nothing else to tell him, she decided to see what she could learn from him. "You have always been the guardian?"

"Nay. I was summoned when the last fulfilled his service and joined the others."

That didn't tell her much. "You have--guarded many maidens?"

"None."

Surprised, Lilith shifted to look at him. "None?"

"You are the only maiden that has passed this way. Young, beautiful women, yes, but not maidens."

"Oh," Lilith responded, disconcerted, mostly because that also didn't answer the question in her mind. It occurred to her after a moment that it was actually an impertinent question to have asked at all. She wasn't even certain why she wanted to know how many women he had initiated into the labyrinth.

"They bring us only the most beautiful." He stopped, thought it over for a moment and then continued looking puzzled, "Or the ugliest and sometimes very old. I have never entirely understood their reasoning."

Lilith stared at him for several moments and finally bit her lip.

He looked intrigued. "What have I said that amuses you?"

"It would be difficult to explain."

"Try."

"They brought me because they thought that I was a witch and they would rid themselves of me by giving me to the demons of the cave. I am certain that is why they bring them all, or at least most."

He frowned but finally dismissed it as of no particular interest. "We do not care so long as they bring them. We have … acquired a taste for mortal women." He glanced down at the tray and picked up another bunch of grapes. "And for the food of mortals."

"Even if they are old and ugly?"

His eyes gleamed at her tone, but he answered seriously. "The old are too frail to entertain us, but, so long as they are willing to serve they are of use."

A shiver skated lightly down Lilith's spine, but, aware of the demon's facility for reading her mind she carefully redirected her thoughts.

He touched her chin, tipping her face up. "You are not as frail as you appear, little bird. Your mother survived. You will also."

Lilith sent him a startled look.

Whether he'd read thoughts she wasn't even conscious of, or he was simply extremely intuitive, Lilith didn't know, but he answered as if he had heard her thoughts. "I did not know her. I was in the nether world when she came. I know she was here because I saw it here," he said, touching the tip of one finger to her temple.

She frowned. "What is the nether world like?" she asked curiously.

His gaze flickered over her face. "Why?"

"I just … wondered. It is hard to imagine what it might be like."

"And you would still not be able to imagine if I told you."

"Oh," she said, vaguely disappointed.

He hesitated and finally placed a palm on either side of her head, closing his eyes. At once images began to burst into her mind of a sprawling, arid wasteland of red stone with only a bit of brown-green vegetation here and there and no trees. The sky was dark with angry clouds that were split again and again with bright blue flashes of light. Fire erupted from the ground from time to time, like fountains except that they spewed molten rock. Sprouting from the parched earth, however, were great palaces with many sharp spires reaching into the sky like jagged teeth. They gleamed and twinkled in the light of the blazing sun in the distance, like precious jewels.

"Oh!" Lilith gasped in awe just before blackness

descended over her like a clap of thunder.

When she opened her eyes again, Gaelen's frowning face swam immediately into view. Lifting a hand to her pounding head, she massaged it. "What happened?"

"Your mind darkened."

Lilith blinked at the harshness of his voice. "I fainted?"

Something flickered in his eyes. "Faint?"

"Blacked out."

"You do this often?" he demanded, his expression a mixture of indignation and something she might have considered anxiety if he had been human.

Lilith thought it over, but she couldn't remember ever fainting before. "No."

"Do not do it again. I do not like it." He set her aside and rose abruptly, taking the tray and stalking from the room.

Still feeling more than a little woozy, Lilith watched his departure in confusion. When he did not come back, she sat up, wondering if it was safe to allow her thoughts to wander at will, or if he could 'read' them even from a distance. She discovered it wasn't really a matter of choice. She couldn't seem to sort through her feelings about anything that had happened. It was almost as if her mind had shut her away from them, almost as if everything had happened to someone else.

The twinges of her body told her otherwise. She *had* been a maiden, and her body was not accustomed to being used to pleasure a man, but she was certainly not ignorant about mating or shocked that he had used her for his pleasure. She knew men did. She had certainly understood the mechanics of it most of her life. She had many animals, and they did not care a snap if she was around or not. If they decided to mount, they did.

She wasn't quite certain of what he was doing, or why. She felt, though, that it was more than merely enjoying his position as guardian.

He had said the demons would expect to entertain

themselves with her. She shivered at the thought, but it also occurred to her to wonder, if he had meant that they would couple with her, why she had any reason to be concerned. It might not be pleasant, but surely there could not be a question of not surviving the 'entertainment'?

The answer seemed unavoidable. He had said he was being gentle with her. He knew the others would not.

Realizing that she was only scaring herself, she got up and went to relieve herself and then wandered down to drink from the cold water near the pool. After staring at the bubbling pool for several moments, she glanced around the cavern. There was little to see beyond rock and more rock.

Except that there was a passage on the other side of the pool.

She stared at it, wondering if there was any possibility at all that she could find her way out of the maze of corridors and caverns. The likelihood seemed great that she couldn't. She'd been blindfolded when he brought her in.

Escape teased at her, but the thoughts of retaliation if she should be caught tamped the budding urge to try. The labyrinth was filled with many demons. She thought, as demons went, that she preferred to stay with the Hawkin.

She realized after a moment that she was staring at the water in the pool. It had felt good and she knew the heat would soothe her aching body. Was she allowed to, though?

She did *not* want to anger Gaelen. She didn't know if he was being gentle with her because he was supposed to, or because he was simply inclined to be because he thought of her as fragile, but she had a feeling that he could be terrifying if she crossed him.

After a few moments' indecision, she moved to the pool anyway and climbed in, allowing the soothing, heated water to wash over her until she began to feel so relaxed she felt heavy. Climbing out again took more of an effort than she would've thought and a wave of dizziness washed over her. Deciding she'd gotten too hot, she crossed to the cold water, splashing it over her face and then drinking her fill.

When she turned, she nearly jumped out of her skin, discovering that Gaelen was watching her and wondering just how long he had been there.

"Come."

Her belly clenched immediately at his tone, for she knew by now what that tone meant, but she didn't dare try to run. Nodding jerkily, she went to him. He caught her hand as she reached him, leading her toward the bed. All of the strength seemed to leave her, especially her legs, and it took an effort to keep from wilting into a puddle on the floor. He surprised her again. Instead of pushing her into the bed, he sat down on the edge. Spreading his legs, he pulled her between them. Wrapping his arms around her, he dragged her close, covering the tip of her breast with his mouth. Heat surged through her instantly as he began to suckle and lick it as he had her woman's place. She swayed dizzily, trying to hold herself up, but sagging more and more heavily against his arms. She could scarcely breathe for the pounding of her heart. When she'd begun to think she would black out from the lack of air, he lifted his mouth and moved to her other breast, suckling the tender nipple until she began to groan and ache with need.

She nearly wilted to the floor when he lifted his head. He caught her face in one hand. "This lesson may be more difficult, but it is one you must learn."

Dazed, her body sizzling from the heat he'd generated in her belly, Lilith merely stared at him uncomprehendingly. "You will pleasure me as I pleasured you before, milking me until you have drained my seed."

Lilith blinked, her gaze moving from his face to his cock.

Saliva pooled in her mouth and she swallowed with an effort, realizing the thought of doing what he said made her feel even more needy. Before she could kneel, he lay back on the bed and dragged her on top of him. Turning her so that her back was to him, he spread her legs until she was straddling his ribs.

She stared at his swollen member for several moments and finally leaned down to take him into her mouth. He was huge. She had thought he was huge when he was thrusting the great thing into her passage, but she could barely open her mouth wide enough to take him in and at that little more than the knob at the end. She sucked on it experimentally feeling a rush of heat, feeling her belly tighten as it had before. Discovering that it gave her pleasure as well as him, she began to suck more feverishly, alternately licking the slick knob of flesh. He took one of her hands and wrapped it tightly around his shaft, guiding it up and down until she grasped the rhythm he wanted.

After a few moments, he caught her hips, drawing her back until she was lying on his belly, and then seized her thighs and pushed them wide, lifting her upward. She jumped when she felt his mouth cover her sex, but as he began to tease her flesh, a fever seemed to grip her and she worked her mouth over him with more fervor.

Another jolt went through her when she felt him push his finger into her rectum, this one not quite as pleasant. She stiffened, trying to pull away. He held her tightly, sucking the bud of flesh and pressing his finger into her rhythmically until the discomfort eased and she felt the stroke of his finger along a place inside of her that rapidly spiraled her body toward climax. Feeling it rushing upon her, she suckled his turgid flesh and stroked him with the desperation of her own need, groaning as the wave of bliss broke over her in pounding waves.

His cock jerked, began to pump his seed into her mouth. She choked, trying to draw away, but he grasped her head and it flickered through her mind that he had said she had to milk him of his seed. Obediently, she swallowed, sucking him until his cock ceased to jerk and finally became flaccid.

Gasping for breath, she dropped her head weakly against his thigh. He lay perfectly limp beneath her for many moments and finally grabbed her arm, dragging her around and flipping her onto her back on the bed beside him. She felt his gaze on her, but now that the fever had subsided, she was discomfited by her enthusiastic reaction to his tutelage and could not bring herself to open her eyes until he sat up and moved to the edge of the bed.

Anxiety swamped her abruptly, for there was something about his attitude that told her he was displeased. "I did not do it right?"

He didn't glance at her. "Yes," he said harshly.

Yes, she did? Or yes, she did not do it right, she wondered worriedly.

If she could not please him, did she have any chance of pleasing the others and winning her freedom?

"I will try again," she said anxiously.

He slid a narrow eyed glance at her. Rising abruptly, he left.

Chapter Four

Lilith had worried over Gaelen's abrupt departure until she was nigh sick with it before he reappeared. At another time, she might have wondered at her need for him and her anxiety for his approval. She had been with him no more than a handful of days, and despite the intimacy between them, he was still very much a stranger to her. Her very life depended upon him, however. She did not want to die in this place and Gaelen had become her safe harbor, her life line. Without him, without his willingness to care for her and guide her, she might or might not have a future. With his help, she knew her chances were far better, though. And she was determined that whatever she had to do to survive, she could and would do it. She knew she could. Her mother had faced this, as Gaelen had pointed out, and she had survived. She was determined that she would, too.

He was angry with her when he returned, but for the life of her she could not fathom why. He *had* been pleasured. She had done exactly what he had told her to do. She could not help it if she did not know how to do it well. She was trying to learn.

She began to be both frightened and angry when he said nothing, scarcely looking at her. "You think I will not please them," she said finally.

He slid a glance at her. "You will."

That sounded both ominous and cryptic, not like a vote of confidence, possibly because he still looked angry. "I have not had much time to learn," she said a little testily, willing anger to her aid to dispel the desire to cry like a frightened child.

He sent her another glance. "You know all that you need

to know."

Shivering at the coldness in his voice, she retreated into silence. After a while, the worry seemed to drain what little energy she had and she slept.

A clatter woke her sometime later. Rousing sleepily, she pushed herself up and looked around. Gaelen, she saw, had dropped a tray of food on the table. Disoriented, with no idea whether it was morning or evening, or how many days had passed since she had been taken into the labyrinth, she threw her legs over the edge of the bed and got up as Gaelen left her alone again.

He appeared again when she had taken care of her needs and eaten. Summoning her with the crook of one finger, he led the way down to the pool. Lilith brightened immediately, felt her body begin to hum with anticipation. He bathed her as before, and returned her to stand beside the brazier as before to dry. She heard him lift the lid of the trunk as she stood drying in front of the heat, and turned curiously.

He held a length of chain in his hands that was the same in size as that which he had threaded through the rings in her nipples and the bud of her sex. Approaching her, he pushed her hair behind her shoulders and fastened the chain to a link on the collar around her neck. When he stepped away, he pulled on the end of the chain in his hand experimentally. Lilith gasped as she felt the tug on the rings embedded in her flesh, felt waves of sensation washing through her.

Wrapping the chain around his hand, he tugged harder, until she moved toward him instinctively to ease the pressure. Apparently satisfied, he dropped the chain, allowing it to drag the floor, and returned to the chest. When he turned to her again, she saw that he was holding manacles linked together. Confusion washed over her as he grasped her wrists, pulled them behind her back and fastened the cuffs.

His expression was taut as he bent and pulled a strip of linen from the chest and then grasped the chain, winding it around his hand. "You have been summoned."

Lilith gaped at him in stunned surprise, but he merely turned away and, tugging at the chain, led her from the room and into the room with the pool. Passing it, he headed toward the opening Lilith had noticed the day before and down a long corridor virtually identical to the one he'd led her down when he had first brought her.

The tug on her tender flesh was insistent as she followed him, impossible to ignore, at times painful when she stumbled. She kept up the best she could, trying to maintain her balance, trying to fight down the growing fear forming tightly around her heart, for the shock of his abrupt announcement had been so profound that she had not been able to wrap her mind around it at first. She did not know why, but she had begun to accept the situation as it was, expected that she would have some warning before he turned her over to the other demons.

Had he not warned her because he was angry with her, she wondered? Or had he been so angry that he would have to give her up that he had not thought to warn her that the time had come when she must face the ordeal that she couldn't begin to imagine lay before her?

She was panting for breath by the time he halted, as much from fear as from exertion. Grasping her arm, he dragged her around and placed the length of linen he had brought with him over her eyes, tying it tightly.

Immediately, Lilith's fear deepened. He caught her shoulders, squeezing them hard enough that it penetrated her fear fogged mind. "I have left no part of your body untouched … and neither will they, but you will not be afraid because I have shown you that you can find pleasure."

Lilith swallowed with an effort, nodding her head jerkily instead of telling him she *was* afraid and asking him why he had blindfolded her.

*Because some things are more fearful when you see them.
There are demons among the horde that you would find
frightening to look upon ... or repulsive. You will not think
of that, though. You will open yourself to the pleasure I
have taught your body and you will be rewarded with it
even as they take pleasure for themselves.*

There was a tug on the chain at almost the same moment
that Gaelen's hands dropped from her shoulders. Confused,
Lilith didn't react at once. She was sorry she hadn't, for the
second jerk was painful. Yielding to the pull, knowing that
Gaelen was no longer guiding her, Lilith stumbled blindly
along, guided only by the pull. She felt the heat of bodies
moving close, heard sounds of movement that told her she
was in a room filled with many creatures, and then her arms
were grasped and she was lifted clear of the floor and
carried. Pain shot through her shoulders and elbows at the
pressure. She bit her lip, trying to focus her mind away
from it, but she was relieved when they set her on her feet
again.

Hands touched her, stroking her body all over and she
realized she was being examined, studied. After a moment,
she was lifted again. This time, though, her legs were
grabbed as well, and forced to bend. She was placed on
something cold and hard--rock, she realized--on her knees.
A hand examined her cleft and then she felt another digging
into her, peeling the fleshy lips of her sex apart. Something
hard pressed against the mouth of her passage. She gasped
when she felt it, jerking instinctively. When she did,
someone tugged at the chain, sending shafts of both
pleasure and pain through her. She went still, panting as she
felt the hands holding her pressing her downward until her
body slowly began to engulf the rigid shaft.

There was no give to it as there was to Gaelen's flesh,
even when it was thoroughly engorged and she had thought
his man root was as hard as rock.

This felt like rock in truth. Panicking, she forgot what Gaelen had told her and tried to struggle, but they merely held her more tightly and drove her downwards with less regard for her body's resistance. She uttered a cry midway between a gasp and a scream as they impaled her on it, expecting any moment to feel her body tearing apart, to feel pain. Instead, after a few mindless moments she realized that neither had happened and her panic subsided. She felt stretched almost to the point of pain, but no real pain, only discomfort.

She'd just begun to relax fractionally when she felt the hands on her legs again. Grasping them, they pulled them out from under her, straightening them so that her own weight bore her down heavily on the shaft. Her heart skipped several beats as she sank more fully upon the rod, felt it pressing against her womb. The hands moved to her ankles and she felt the coldness of metal clamping around them.

They withdrew, leaving her to sway dizzily, disoriented by the blindfold and off balance. Slowly, the tightness of the muscles along her passage began to ease, but that only allowed the shaft deeper penetration until she began to pant with the discomfort and the fear she refused to acknowledge that it might be plunged deeper still.

A hot mouth covered one nipple. She jumped at the unexpected heat of it and the fierceness of the assault, which was almost as painful as it was pleasurable. Despite that, heat blossomed in her belly and moisture gathered round the shaft. A second mouth covered her other nipple, suckling and nipping at it with sharp teeth so that pain and pleasure alternately rippled through her.

Her breath sawed in and out of her chest raggedly. She swayed for many moments between fear, pleasure and pain, but the incessant tugging at her sensitive nipples began to overwhelm fear and discomfort. Dizziness washed over her as the heat of carnal need enveloped her. Her body clenched and relaxed rhythmically around the shaft until she began to gasp and moan with pleasure.

Abruptly, the shaft began to move downward, sliding along her passage, and then upward again, swiftly impaling her. She gasped, swaying, and teeth clamped over her nipples, bearing down just enough to be threatening, to hold her in place. She went still, held herself upright with an effort as the shaft began to pump into her at a frantic pace, jarringly, but driving her so quickly toward release that it caught her unaware as it pounded through her so hard she thought her heart would explode.

The thrusting continued unabated, driving her body to convulse on and on until she feared she would black out, until her gasps became hoarse screams. Abruptly, the shaft began to jerk and spasm and spew hot seed into her, demolishing the thought that it was not flesh at all.

Her knees gave way when the pleasure wracking her body began to dissipate at last. She came down painfully on the shaft, which she could not tell had diminished in any way. After a brief moment of respite, the thrusting began again. She groaned, but the incessant tugging on her breasts and the stroking along her passage awoke her body once more and the tension began to build in her rapidly again.

When it burst over her the second time, she screamed at the intensity of it, gasping, almost weeping at the hard jerks ripping through her.

Darkness swarmed over her like ants in a stirred anthill, her flesh stinging, twitching. It was woefully brief. It seemed to her that it was not more than a blink and then she woke to a relentless tugging and nibbling at her nipples that forced her body to stir to life, that poured heat through her body into her belly where the tension began to wind again even before the huge cock began pumping into her insistently, with an unyielding determination to wring every ounce of pleasure from her body.

Dazed by the powerful expulsions of passion she'd

already experienced, her senses were sluggish to respond and that only seemed to inspire the beasts to a more ferocious assault. The tempo increased until she reached the point of no return a third time and the convulsions of rapture ripped through her again, tearing hoarse cries from her until the waves ceased to pound through her.

The darkness that swept over her that time seemed more profound. Again she was roused by the tugging at her nipples, but she was so exhausted she merely groaned, her head slumped forward on her shoulders. She wasn't even certain of whether the tugging was from the mouths that seemed to have tormented her forever, or if the tug was from the chains as she wavered back and forth, trying to maintain her balance. Doubt was removed when the tugging failed to yield the expected response and teeth bit into her hard enough to pierce the fog, tearing a hoarse cry from her.

Apparently even that was not response enough, for a mouth, or what felt like a mouth, latched onto her clit and began to tug on it with a ferocity that shot fire through her. The engorged member that no number of releases seemed to diminish began to drive into her almost frenziedly at the same moment. She had been certain moments before that no amount of stimulation could force her body to culminate again, and yet, with a sense of dread, she felt it tightening inside of her within moments, felt the jarring, excruciating waves of exquisite sensation tearing through her again until, thankfully, she knew nothing at all.

She had thought that Gaelen had pushed her in the days she had spent with him, learning the way that she would have to pleasure the demons of the Labyrinth. She found, though, that he had been indeed gentle, had coaxed far more than demanded, certainly in comparison to the others. Even her exhaustion did not deter them, for they only prodded her harder until the culminations themselves were almost torture as they wracked her over and over again.

She had no idea how long they entertained themselves with her, but it began to seem endless and each time she became convinced that they had wrung all from her that they possibly could, they would begin again and show her that she was wrong. Neither did the releases seem to diminish. Instead, each time her body convulsed, it seemed the spasms were harder, that the waves washed over her longer before they began to diminish until she'd begun to black out purely from shortness of breath each time her body seized with convulsions of pleasure until at long last her body did finally reach its limit and she fell into a deep pit of oblivion.

When she became dimly aware of her surroundings again, Lilith realized she was being carried. The effort to lift her head was simply beyond her, however, and after trying a couple of times, she merely hung, limply draped over the arms beneath her shoulders and thighs. She didn't realize the manacles had been removed from her wrists until she felt the unexpected brush of water against her fingers and instinctively jerked away from the heat. She was settled on a hard surface and could feel the heated water lapping at her as she heard the splash of water close at hand. Struggling, she managed to lift one eyelid enough to see that Gaelen stood in the pool next to her, rubbing soap into a cloth.

She gasped when he began to bathe her. As certain as she had been that she was beyond feeling much of anything any longer, she discovered that she was completely wrong. Her skin felt overly sensitive, not numb, and the lightest of touches sent tremors through her, painful echoes of the climaxes that had been wrenched from her over and over until she'd lost count.

He ignored her weak protests, bathing her from head to foot and then pressing her thighs wide and bathing the swollen, bruised nether regions of her body. When he'd finished, he pulled her into the pool and rinsed the lather from her and then carried her out. Apparently realizing she was too weak to dry herself in front of the brazier, he simply placed her on the mattress and wrapped the sheet around her shivering form. Relieved that her trial seemed to be over, at least for a little while, she rolled onto her side, curled into a tight ball and sought oblivion.

She protested when she was roused, but felt herself scooped up anyway and pressed against a hard wall that she realized after a few moments was a chest. Dizzying movement followed and then she realized Gaelen had settled on the bed with her half lying, half sitting across his lap.

Something was pressed to her lips. She turned her head away. He caught her head and turned it back. "Eat," he growled.

She took the bite of food into her mouth, chewing and swallowing, but she had no real idea of what it was and didn't particularly care. The only thing she really wanted to do was to seek oblivion again, but he was persistent in feeding her until he decided she had eaten enough.

When he had set the tray aside, he settled her more comfortably against his shoulder and began to stroke her in a soothing motion that set her mind to wandering lazily. She didn't know if he was doing it to soothe her, either consciously or unconsciously, or it was merely that he liked the feel of her skin beneath his palms. It didn't particularly matter to her one way or the other, however. She found it relaxing and comforting.

She was almost asleep when he ceased to stroke her back and lifted his hand to her head, splaying a palm along one cheek and tipping her head back to look down at her face. "I warned you not to struggle against them," he murmured. "They can feed upon your passion, or upon your pain. They do not particularly care which it is, but fighting them only excites their desire to draw from your pain."

Lilith lifted her heavy eyelids to look up at him dully.

"You watched."

He frowned, but she could see confusion in his eyes. "I did not enjoy it," he said finally, seeming surprised to realize he hadn't.

Curiosity pricked her, tempting her to ask him why he hadn't enjoyed watching when he apparently did in general. She shied away from it, however, not certain why it had even occurred to her to wonder or care.

"Does it matter to you whether it's pleasure or pain?"

Again he seemed to ponder the question. "Yes," he murmured finally, dipping his head to fit his lips lightly to hers in gentle exploration. "I do not want you to feel fear or pain. This is why I tried to prepare you for what was to come."

She gasped in surprise, partly because his mouth was more coaxing than demanding and partly because she couldn't fathom why he had any interest in doing anything so obscurely sexual when he had shown no interest before in doing anything that suggested tenderness and caring rather than carnal need.

The tentativeness of it disarmed her. She found herself kissing him back, warmed by the feel of his mouth on hers, the glide of his tongue. One of her arms was trapped beneath his along his side. She lifted the other, placing her palm over his hard male breast and stroking her hand upward along his chest to his neck.

The touch, light though it was, sent a tremor through him. The timbre of his kiss altered subtly, became more demanding. Cupping her hand around the back of his neck, she stroked upward to the base of his skull and then down again, following the hard ridge of flesh from his neck to his shoulder.

At about the same moment, she realized, dimly, that her light, curious touch, rather than being received as what it was, an offering, appreciation for his gentleness, was driving his urges beyond his control, he tore his lips from hers, tipped her back onto the bed, grasped her thighs and buried his face into her cleft, licking and sucking at the achingly tender flesh with mindless need. She grunted as the air left her lungs as if it had been punched from her chest, trying to grab at his head and thrust him away. He caught her hands, pinning them to the mattress and continued to tug at her until the sensation she'd begun to dread tightened until it seemed every muscle in her body seized.

She screamed hoarsely as the tension snapped and exploded in shattering waves.

She was still struggling to catch her breath when he covered her, driving his engorged member into her. Pain instantly supplanted the ecstasy of moments before. She was raw from such unaccustomed activity, so sore she felt like she couldn't bear it. She began to struggle against him. For several moments, he seemed oblivious, but some of her panic finally communicated itself to him. He stopped abruptly, pulling away enough to stare down at her.

Relief surged through her when he pulled out of her and stepped from the bed. It was short lived. He returned moments later, smearing some sort of cream liberally on his cock. "No," Lilith gasped as he pried her thighs apart and pressed his hard, engorged flesh into her again.

He caught her wrists, pinning them to the bed on either side of her head. "This will soothe and heal," he ground out. "You will suffer more tomorrow if I do not do this."

She desisted, because she knew it was hopeless, not because she believed him. Closing her eyes, she turned her head away, feeling hot tears of weakness and exhaustion trickle down her cheeks. She found after a very few moments, though, that he had not lied only because he was determined to use her body to find release. The cream soothed the burning pain.

She was still glad when he shuddered and went still.

She didn't know why she had thought, hoped, that he was

different from the others. He wasn't. He was a demon as they were and he had no real conception of tenderness, or affection, or caring. Her beasts knew more about affection than the demons. He had only been gentle with her because he was fearful they would break their plaything too quickly and have to wait until the villagers brought them a new one.

Remembering that the villagers were responsible for her plight brought a surge of hate to her such as she had never known. She was sorrier than ever that she was no real witch and did not have the power to punish them for what they'd done to her. She resolved, though, that if she made it out of the labyrinth, she would never go near the village again, not even if they came begging for herbs or potions to heal their sick, which they had on several occasions in the past. They could all die, rot, and go to perdition for all she cared.

* * * *

Dread settled in Lilith's mind as she was led into the chamber she had been led to the day before. Her body had a mind of its own, however, and sent as much excitement surging through her as anxiety, her belly clenching, her passage growing warm and damp in anticipation of the endless pleasure it was already beginning to crave.

Trying to ignore both, Lilith focused on what Gaelen had told her--if she did not submit, she would suffer the consequences, and as hard as it was to endure the stimulation and release over and over, it was still far preferable to the possibility of real pain. She felt like she had a much better chance of surviving the exhausting pleasure than the other.

Despite every effort, she still tensed when they lifted her, knowing what was coming. She focused on relaxing as she felt the fingers parting the flesh of her sex, breathing as slowly and evenly as possible as she was lowered onto the knob of unyielding flesh. A tentative flicker of relief and gratitude washed over her when she discovered the salve Gaelen had forced into her had relieved most of the soreness. She panted to keep her muscles relaxed and yielding as they pulled her legs from under her and her own weight forced the shaft deeper, but she quickly realized she had not really remembered how huge it felt, how impossibly tightly it stretched her body. Her belly clenched almost painfully as they forced it deeper still, tugging at her legs.

When they had finally ceased to pull at her legs, something settled on her shoulders. Surprised at the deviation from the ritual of the day before, Lilith jerked, a ripple of tension rolling through her. The pressure and weight of it increased, bearing down on her until her toes and then the soles of her feet touched the stone floor and the manacles were secured to her ankles.

Confused by the change, she realized after a moment that it not only held her down, it supported her back and head. Relieved that she would at least not to worry that she would hurt herself by losing her balance, she quickly discovered the new device was in no way intended for her comfort. Her head was strapped to it to keep her from drawing backwards.

She was still wondering why when something hard pushed against her lips. Yielding to the pressure, she opened her mouth, closing it again around the cock that was shoved into the cavity. The mouths from the day before, or different mouths, latched onto her nipples hungrily and began to tug and pull at them, sending radiating heat through her and into her belly even as the shaft began to pump into her passage. She worked her mouth over the cock that was thrusting into her, at first only because she knew it was expected of her.

As the pleasurable tension began building inside of her, though, her hunger grew and she began to suck on it as feverishly as the demons tugged on her nipples. She was so intent with the pleasure building inside of her she scarcely noticed when the turgid flesh began to jerk and spew salty liquid down her throat. By that time her own crisis was upon her and she hardly knew where she was, sucking on it almost aggressively as her body was rocked with shockwave after shockwave of undiluted bliss.

Afterward, she was allowed to rest until her breathing was more or less normal again. She realized then that the bondage was not merely for the sake of control. They were taking turns pleasuring themselves with her and too impatient to wait. They had bound her so that more than one at the time could entertain themselves with her flesh.

It was almost a relief to realize that she wasn't servicing one insatiable demon, but several--she thought. She could not be certain, for she was blindfolded still and had no idea what form these demons had. Still, hope filled her that she would more rapidly be done and allowed to leave.

If she could only endure a little longer, she added as a mental after thought as she felt them begin to tug her body to life once more and the process was repeated.

The hopefulness did not outlast the day. She hadn't realized that they had been 'gentle' the day before in their use. When her body had expended itself to the point that she began to faint with weakness each time she was forced over the edge again, they merely worked harder to drag more from her. Eventually she reached the point that even the hard nipping with teeth on her nipples failed to elicit much of a response, but they merely abandoned that avenue of stimulation and began to work on her pleasure bud with equal enthusiasm until they had her screaming again with the force of her release.

As before, time seemed to hang upon her. She could not focus her mind beyond what they were doing to her, beyond the sensations that poured through her with each coupling, and they would not allow it even if she had tried. She thought, though, that she was bound far longer than the day before, forced to culminate until her entire body felt like it had no consistency or substance and she finally reached a point of exhaustion where they could not touch her anymore.

She awakened to find herself at the bathing pool--or *a* bathing pool. She found it difficult to tell one part of the labyrinth from another, mostly, she supposed, because she had had little opportunity to actually study her surroundings. She didn't try to protest the touching required to bathe her as she had the day before, knowing it was as useless to object to that as anything else and deciding to save her energies for more critical expenditures.

Neither did she protest when Gaelen carried her back into the room, dried her with the linen, and cuddled her against his chest to feed her. She turned her face away, however, when he tried to kiss her. She wasn't falling for *that* again! She had never considered herself a complete fool, but she'd begun to feel like one. The villagers had terrorized her, and her fear of the labyrinth had been almost as great. It was small wonder that she had latched onto Gaelen's offer to protect her as if it was a lifeline, but she still felt like an idiot for believing anything told to her by a demon. The truth, to them, was whatever served the purpose, or the moment.

Her throat closed at the thought, because she had needed so badly to feel even a small sense of security and now she had been deprived of even that illusion. Deep down, she supposed she had realized all along that his agenda was not necessarily her own. He had not tried to lie about that. He had told her straight out that his duty was to see to it that she was taken care of. It was unreasonable to be angry and disappointed because he had failed to meet her expectations, but she couldn't help but be anyway, anymore than she could have stopped herself from wanting to believe the lie she'd concocted for herself to begin with.

He would not accept her rebuff, but then she had not really believed he would. She had only meant for him to know that she was not giving. He was taking.

She remained stubbornly passive as he kissed her, even though she felt the lure to yield to his persuasion, keeping her hand carefully tucked against her. He looked baffled and angry when he pulled away. "It is not the same."

She flicked a glance at him from beneath her lashes. "Taking never is."

She made no attempt to shield herself from his gaze as he tipped her onto her back, but she couldn't prevent herself from tensing when he looked down at her sex hungrily.

After what seemed an endless moment of time, he slipped from the bed and took the salve, lavishing it along his member. Lilith watched him, torn between a vague disappointment that he had not pleasured her with his mouth and another emotion that seemed equal parts triumph that he had felt the rebuff and irritation, that he apparently had no intention of allowing that to put him off finding his own release.

She found her conflicting emotions baffling. Unreasonable or not, the hurt and anger, she understood. She even understood the desire to wound him in return. Why she felt both disappointed and gratified that he had decided not to concern himself with her pleasure confused her, as did the vaguely acknowledged desire for him to wound her more so she could hate him better.

It occurred to her that the last was self-preservation. The more quickly he thoroughly disillusioned her, the less she would expect of him and the less she would be hurt in the long run.

Theoretically.

That depended, of course, on how deeply her emotions ran and she could not determine that with any certainty. She was still trying to sort through reality and the things she had allowed herself to think.

She tensed when he climbed onto the bed and brushed his cock head down her cleft, wincing as he pushed slowly inside of her. He ignored her distress, bracing his palms on her wrists, even though she had made no attempt to elude him or to fight. Her fingers curled into her palms when he succeeded in driving to her core. She caught her breath and held it as he slid slowly out and then returned, trying to relax the tension in her body.

To her surprise, instead of thrusting with a faster and faster pace, after slowly gliding in and out of her several times, he went perfectly still. When she opened her eyes to look up at him, she saw that his face was contorted as if in pain. Slowly, he withdrew--completely.

Settling beside her, he lay staring at the uneven rock ceiling above them for several moments and finally slipped an arm around her and dragged her against his side, stroking his hand down her back. "Only one day more," he said after a few moments, "and then they will allow you to rest for three days."

The first words from his mouth had brought a flicker of hope that died a painfully swift death.

"I do not understand mortals," he said finally. "You are given pleasure for the pleasure taken. How could you not want it?"

Lilith frowned, realizing that that was another point of confusion that she was having trouble sorting out. The truth was, she had begun to crave it--or at least her body had--to hunger for the release they gave her even while she dreaded it because it was nearly unbearable to feel so much.

"They all do."

Lilith glanced at him in surprise. "They?"

"The mortal women brought to us. That is why they stay, because they crave our touch as much as we hunger for theirs."

It took many moments for that to sink in, mostly because she had believed--as everyone did--that those who never returned didn't because they weren't allowed to, or they died. "The women who have been brought to you?"

"Yes."

The relief was so profound, her eyes and nose stung with tears. "I will be allowed to go?"

She saw when he turned to study her face that his eyes were tumultuous with emotion. "In time. If you wish."

Lilith smiled, her heart racing with excitement. "Yes. I wish it."

His eyes narrowed. "You are not concerned that the villagers will harm you?"

"Oh," Lilith said, feeling her euphoria promptly dashed. "I expect I will have to move away," she added after a moment, trying not to think about all the years she and her mother had put into the cottage in the woods to make it comfortable.

"If you can not return to your home, why would you want to go?"

She frowned. "I miss my forest--the sky, the trees, the animals. They need me. They always come to me when they are sick or hurt. If I am not there to care for them, no one will, and they will die."

"You will miss the fire in your blood, the passion only we can give you."

Lilith shivered. She wanted to deny it, categorically, but she thought in some ways that she would. Before, she was entirely content with no one. She had thought, one day, that perhaps she would have a child, but she had not even considered then that she would live with a man and, even if she had, she would only have thought of one--not many. "One can not have everything," she said finally, "and I think if I must give up one or the other I will be happier in my forest."

Chapter Five

As accustomed as Lilith was to staying busy from daylight to dark to maintain her home in the forest, she might have been bored in the time she was given to rest except that she slept more than she was awake. It wasn't until the end of the second day that she finally noticed that Gaelen watched her whenever he was in the room with her with a mixture of hunger, baffled anger, and what she might have interpreted as concern if he had not been what he was.

She was too weary in the beginning to give any thought to the fact that he made no attempt to couple with her except to think that she was glad for the respite from sexual congress of any sort. By the third day, however, she began to wonder why he merely stared at her with hunger in his eyes and remained angry and aloof.

The only explanation that presented itself seemed too farfetched to consider, but she could not help but wonder if her rejection had gone deeper than she would have thought possible. It was not that she did not think he was capable of any of the more human emotions--he certainly had no trouble with anger--but she had come to think the denizens of the labyrinth were more basic and far less complex creatures than humans where emotion was concerned. Not like dumb beasts, certainly, for she had found that most were capable of a good deal of affection, but perhaps somewhere between the human and the creatures of the forests and fields?

She was intrigued, but not enough to let down her guard again, particularly now that she had come to realize that the demons would free her once they had satiated themselves with her.

He might have lied to her about that, she knew, but it was the only hope she had to hold onto and she clung to it determinedly, refusing to allow her mind to examine the offer for fear that she might find flaws in it that would mean it *was* a lie.

As hard as she had tried to convince herself that she detested the things they did to her, she had already begun to feel a mixture of dread and anticipation when Gaelen took her to the pool the night before she was to be summoned again. She was so focused on it, in fact, that she didn't realize that Gaelen had deviated from his typical routine when he first settled her on the stone. He had bathed her with the same slow, careful thoroughness as ever, and rinsed the lather from her. Instead of leaving the pool, however, and leading her to the brazier to dry herself, he took her legs one at the time and lifted her foot to the ledge.

Her stomach clenched at the intent she saw in his gaze as he pushed her legs wide. His cock, she saw, was erect, so engorged the skin was shiny with the strain. His gaze moved from her face to her sex and he brushed the fingers of one hand lightly over her nether lips, parting them, stroking her cleft.

Heat instantly pooled in her belly at his touch. Her mouth went dry.

He began to stroke his engorged member with one hand as he studied her pink flesh intently, touching her lightly with fingers that trembled noticeably. Thoroughly aroused, she found her breath hitching in her chest as she watched him. Anticipation gathered inside of her in heated, moist welcome.

After a few moments, he placed a palm on the stone beside her and leaned close, so close she could feel the heat of his breath, felt almost as if her skin reached out to him the way it prickled and grew more sensitive. His breathing grew ragged as he began to stroke himself faster. His face contorted as if with pain.

He leaned away after a moment, examining her sex again, carefully separating the thin, sensitive petals of flesh, stroking them with the fingers of one hand as he continued to stroke himself with the other.

Confusion began to usurp the sense of excitement humming through her when he made no attempt to enter her. She could not bring herself to ask him to possess her, but she found herself arching her hips upward as he stroked her, trying to coax him to pleasure her. Her heartbeat and breath seemed to keep pace with his as he grew closer and closer to release. Abruptly, he uttered a wrenching groan, caught himself by bracing his palm on the stone again and pumped his seed from his body.

Lilith found her gaze was glued to his member as it jerked, expelling a milky substance. For several moments after the convulsions had stopped, he leaned near her, his huge body shaking, quivering, and then he pushed away abruptly and left her beside the pool.

Feeling strangely let down, achy, incomplete, Lilith watched his departure in stunned disbelief.

From out of no where the urge to cry descended over her when he had disappeared from her view. She could not begin to sort through the chaotic emotions tumbling through her, however, and after a while, when she had managed to master the urge, she got up and went into the room.

Gaelen was not there and disappointment washed over her all over again, banishing the half formed hope that perhaps he was waiting for her there, ousting the heated images that had swarmed her mind of Gaelen pushing her roughly onto the mattress and driving into her until she was screaming with her release. After standing for some time before the brazier, wondering if he would come, she finally realized he had no intention of doing so and climbed into the bed, pulled the cover over herself and tried to compose herself for sleep.

Her efforts went largely unrewarded. Quite apart from the fact that her body still sizzled and complained from unappeased arousal, there was a sense of disquiet and unhappiness about the situation that went far deeper. Was this some sort of punishment for her rejection? Or did he simply not consider it worth the effort to try to change her mind?

As bad as she hated to admit it, even to herself, he would have found it woefully easy to break through her pathetic defenses. She *was* hurt. She *was* angry, but she desperately wanted reassurance from him and she would have caved in at once if he'd only come to her with the same gentleness and hunger of before.

When Gaelen woke her the following morning, she staggered drunkenly from the bed and went to relieve herself and then to wash. She felt little better when she returned, but more alert. Gaelen had left food for her--left it, for he had disappeared again.

Her stomach knotted. She was summoned today. Immediately, the mixture of dread and anticipation that she'd felt the night before returned. Between that and her distress over Gaelen's behavior, she found it hard to eat even a little.

When he returned, he glanced at the tray, but said nothing. Instead, he withdrew a harness of some sort from the chest and motioned for her to stand. When she stood up, he bade her step into the leather loops and then moved the device up to her hips and fastened it around her waist. Lilith looked down at the harness in puzzlement. It was no garment certainly, for it was made up entirely of straps, and yet it fit snugly along the tops of her thighs and around her waist.

She could not imagine its purpose.

She did not have to wonder long, however. He told her to sit again on the edge of the bed and pushed her down onto her back. Bending her knees, he lifted her feet to the bed and pushed her thighs wide. Removing something else from the chest, he returned to the bed and knelt. She saw then that he had two strange looking metal clamps. When he pinched one edge together, the other end opened like a wide beak. Catching one side of her fleshy nether lips, he attached the clamping devise and then attached the opposite end of the clamp to the strap around one thigh. Lilith winced at the pinch of the metal, but it was more uncomfortable than painful. Within a very few moments, however, the blood began to pulse in the flesh he had clamped. Lilith was still wondering if it would grow more than uncomfortable when he caught the other lip of her sex and repeated the process.

After studying his handiwork for a moment, he placed a palm on each of her knees and slowly pushed them wider. The tug increased the discomfort but not unbearably so.

She didn't have to see to know the purpose. The moment he spread her thighs wide she felt a caress of chilling air on the tender flesh exposed by the device. The muscles along her passage clenched in response, grew moist with expectation.

Apparently satisfied, he dragged her feet from the bed, caught her wrist and pulled her up.

He studied her for several moments and finally took her wrists and bound them behind her back. When he had blindfolded her, he caught her arm and led her from the room.

Bound as she was, it was difficult to walk. It was even more difficult to take her mind off of her sex and the summons. She could not expect more of the same, she realized, feeling a touch of dismay, for she had grown at least somewhat accustomed to the other.

She knew when they entered the room where the demons had gathered to feast upon her flesh. Gaelen pulled her to a halt and then released her, leaving her to stand alone.

A moment later, she heard someone approach, felt their presence nearby. The tinkle of the chain alerted her moments before she felt the tug as a hand grasped the chain attached to her collar and tugged, commanding her wordlessly to follow. When the pulling stopped, a hand grasped her waist and another pushed on her shoulders, forcing her to bend over until she felt something cold and hard pressing against her chest. She was nudged forward until her breasts were hanging free of whatever it was beneath her. The hand that had forced her to bend over moved to the middle of her back and held her.

She could hear movements and an odd assortment of noises, but she could tell nothing about how many were in the room with her or what they were doing. Something cold, and similar to the piece beneath her breasts, was pressed against the top of her breasts. It tightened and continued to tighten until Lilith grew tense. It took an effort to prevent herself from trying to jerk away from the tightening. She was shaking when it finally stopped, panting for breath.

As with the flesh of her sex, the tightening around her breasts made the blood pool and throb at the tips, bringing them to a heavy, aching sensitivity in moments. Her nipples tightened, stood erect, pulsing even harder than the rest of her breasts. She was still trying to catch her breath when hands grasped her legs. Forcing them to bend, they tilted her upward slightly and then pulled her legs wide, so wide the tug between them began to skate the edge of pain. Her knees were settled on something hard and then clamped in place. She couldn't fall, but neither could she support the weight of her hips with her legs spread so wide and yet each time she relaxed and settled lower, the clamps on her nether lips tugged her sex wider.

She heard the sound of movement again and then a mouth clamped over her breast, greedily tugging and sucking at it. A wash of heat went through her. A second wave joined the first as another mouth caught her other nipple. Dizzy with the pleasure shooting through her, she dropped her head forward, struggling to breathe, making no attempt to stem the tide of heated desire that began to coil tightly inside of her. A moment later she felt a brush along her belly that made it quiver and a hot mouth covered her clit, tugging and sucking at it. She moaned, finding within moments that she could not be still beneath the assault, nor move more than a fraction of an inch in any direction. She was so deeply sunk in pleasurable agony she hardly noticed the hands on her buttocks until they spread the cheeks wide. Something hard and rounded pressed against the mouth of her sex, spreading the flesh wide as it penetrated her passage. A moment later, a second shaft, this one smaller than the first, pressed against her rectum. She gasped, trying to buck. Hands grasped her hips, tightening, forcing both shafts deeply inside of her and then withdrawing almost at once, ramming into her harder the second time, faster the third. She groaned as pleasure and pain warred within her, mingled, seemed to heighten sensation all together.

A hand tangled in her hair, dragging her head back and a cock was shoved into her mouth. Half mad with the exquisite sensations pounding through her, she closed her mouth on the rounded head, sucking and licking it with the desperation she felt building inside of her. The eruption that burst inside of her within only a few moments was terrific, explosive. Encompassed in a fire storm of ecstasy, she sucked as greedily at the cock in her mouth as it began to jerk and twitch and spill its seed as the mouths sucked her breasts and clit, as frenziedly as the pounding double penetration inside of her passages.

She was reluctant to let go when the member was withdrawn, but even as she dragged in a deep shuddering breath, another was pushed into her mouth. And as the frantic thrusting in her sex jerked, grew still, and then withdrew, she was penetrated again.

With no time for her body to cool, the quaking never actually stopped. It merely quieted and then her body began to build again toward release. The tugging at her breasts and clit stopped for several moments and then began again as new, hungry mouths, took the place of those before.

Without sight, her mind struggled to imagine the unimaginable, conjuring dark figures surrounding her, penetrating her body with frenzied need even as other shadowy forms jostled for a taste of her, tugging and suckling her tender flesh.

She climaxed over and over until abruptly everything went black. She was still gasping when she was dragged back to awareness by the unremitting feeding upon her, forced to culmination so many times in rapid succession that it all seemed to blend together, her body shuddering and convulsing endlessly until everything would abruptly shut down in blackness and then she was brought round again.

She began to feel that she could take no more, feel no more, but the blood continued to pound through her, rapture cresting explosively and then almost immediately beginning to build toward another release. For hour upon hour, or so it seemed, her breasts and clit continued as acutely sensitive and responsive to the relentless pulling and tugging as they had begun. And when, after a time, her response became more sluggish, they left her as she was for a time, only to begin all over again, sucking upon her fingers and toes until her body began to quake with renewed sensation and then transferring to her nipples and clit again to drag more pleasure from her. She moaned and cried out with each shattering release until she was screaming hoarsely and still it went on until she could no longer scream at all and finally felt nothing at all.

She could not contain a whimper of pain as she was pulled at last from the bindings and lifted against a hard chest. Weary past bearing, she dropped her head to his hard shoulder, knowing it was Gaelen who held her. The bath was nearly as tortuous, for her body still ached and twitched and jerked at the slightest touch.

He settled in the bed with her on his lap, pressing food against her lips. She compressed them.

"Eat!" he growled.

"Not hungry," she whispered hoarsely.

"Eat anyway."

She managed to send him a cross look, but she took the food and chewed it. After several bites, she discovered that some of the weakness had left her and that she felt more alert, still weary almost past bearing, but more aware. "You wanted me last night," she whispered after a few moments, remembering what he'd done.

He said nothing for several moments. Finally, almost as if he were trying to pick apart a puzzle that had been plaguing him for some time, he responded. "I always want you," he muttered in his deep, rumbling voice. "It is a fire in my brain and loins that will not be extinguished."

She glanced up at him in surprise, whereupon he shoved a grape into her mouth.

Frowning, she chewed it. "But you did not ... do anything."

He sent her an angry look. "I took care of my need. It eased the pain of want."

"The others take," she said tentatively.

His face twisted in anger. Scooping her off his lap abruptly, he plunked her down on the bed. Grabbing the tray of food, he dropped it to the floor with a clatter that spilled much of the remaining food over the edges. Ignoring the mess, he stalked to the chest and removed the cream he had used before to soothe her sex.

When he returned to the bed, he knelt, dipped a finger into the cream, pushed her legs apart and thrust his finger into her sex, stroking it along the walls of her passage until he had thoroughly coated it. Removing his finger after a moment, he scooped up another glob and pushed his finger into her rectum.

When he had finished, he tossed the jar in the general direction of the chest, turned, and stalked from the room. A little stunned by his fit of temper, Lilith stared at his back until he disappeared and finally settled down on the bed and curled beneath the covers. She was far too exhausted to ponder his behavior, however. She was asleep even before she found a comfortable position.

She roused a little later to feel his heat against her. He draped an arm across her, dragging her more snugly against his belly and finally settled. Surprised, but glad for his comforting warmth, Lilith snuggled against him and drifted away again.

As tired as Lilith was each morning as Gaelen led her to the beasts, she discovered that each day she felt less dread and more anticipation. Even as she went about her morning ritual of preparation, her blood began to sing in her veins. The first tug on the chain sent currents through her breasts and clit, stirring her body to life, and as she was positioned for their pleasure and bound, she grew breathless with excitement, warm, wet. The feel of their mouths and hands and teeth all over body, the unrestrained, often almost violent pounding of their engorged flesh into her body's orifices seemed to build a hunger for more each time they forced her into the intense explosions of release.

They will leave no part of you unexplored, Gaelen had told her. At the time she had found that frightening, even though he had gently guided her through her first knowledge of what that entailed. In time, she began to look forward to each new experience. Sometimes the things they did to her skated the edge of pain, and sometimes it moved beyond that barrier, but each time they would bring her to release the discomfort seemed to intensify the pleasure.

She was in no state during the time they took their

pleasure from her to think. The focus of her entire world had narrowed to the unremitting stimulation of her senses. When she was allowed a few days to rest and recover, however, she found she mended much faster than before. After sleeping for the better part of a day and half, she woke to a nameless restlessness.

Gaelen, she finally realized, had taken to avoiding her, disappearing for longer and longer periods of time. At first she thought it was because he had ceased to concern himself that she might try to escape. When she finally realized, though, that he only came to perform the duties assigned to him, she began to wonder what he did when he left her.

The demons, from what she could tell, were creatures of the flesh. They had no need to toil as humans did for survival and comfort, for they had their powers to ensure that there was food when they wanted it, fire for warmth and cooking. They seemed to spend most of their days focusing only on feeding their appetite for carnal pleasures.

So what did Gaelen do when he was not with her? For that matter, what did he do instead of easing himself on her? Except for the incident in the pool, which had been nigh a week earlier, she had no firsthand knowledge of him seeking release. She had been with him for weeks, long enough to know that his appetite for pleasure was as keen as the other demons, for even though he had taken care to go slowly with her at first, initiating her with patience to every facet of appeasing desire, she had also had the sense that he was only waiting until he thought she could receive him again without harm.

Thinking back, she realized that, even in the beginning, he had not seemed to have any difficulty curbing his appetite. He had told her he always wanted her, that she was a fire in his brain and body, but he did not act as if that was true. He had not taken her as the others did, with a complete disregard for her human frailty, which she would have expected if he had been so needy of feasting upon her passion.

Was he *that* different from the others, she wondered?

Or was it that he appeased his hunger elsewhere?

That thought sent an unpleasant, chaotic jolt of emotions through her.

He had said there were other human women among them. Did he go to them to appease his hunger?

Or had the people brought yet another 'sacrifice' to the beasts of the cave? Was he teaching her even now in the ways of the flesh? Taming her fears by lavishing her with his gentle ministrations?

He had been chosen as guardian, she realized abruptly, because he *was* different from the others. In many ways, probably not so very different, but different in the one way that mattered most. Like her, he understood the creatures in the world beyond his own, sensed their needs and knew how to handle them, to gentle and tame so that they would grow accustomed and cease to struggle in fear.

His task had been given to him because he was willing, and capable, of making certain the others, in their enthusiasm and total disregard for the frailty of humans, did not destroy their gift and none of the others had that self-control or understanding.

When she had grown hurt and angry because she had realized none of the things he had done arose from any real caring for her and turned away from him, had he merely dismissed her and turned his attentions to one he thought needed it more? Had it not bothered him at all?

She frowned at the direction of her thoughts. Pushing the covers back, she rose from the bed and took care of her needs. Gaelen had appeared in the opening to the corridor when she returned from bathing herself.

"Today we move on again," he said in the deep, rumbling voice that carried little inflection of emotion.

She was a little surprised by the announcement, partly

because she didn't realize they had moved before. Everything looked much the same as the first place they had stopped, but she supposed she either hadn't really been in any state to notice a great deal or the many rooms were simply furnished identically.

Nodding, she followed him. As before, he led her past the pool and into another long corridor that opened beyond it. She was not as stiff and sore as she had been before, not as frightened, not as bone weary, and she glanced around with curiosity. There was little to see for all that. The corridor varied little that she could see from the others they had traversed. She realized after a time, however, that whereas the others had seemed to gradually dip lower and lower into the bowels of the earth, this one reached a point after a while where it began to climb.

She heard the sound of voices and trickling water after a while. The sounds became more pronounced as they progressed and finally they stepped into a wide cavern. In this cavern, she saw a heated, bubbling pool much like the others, except that this was many times bigger.

There were women lounging around the perimeter, fat, thin and in between, young, old and in between, all naked just as she was, except they bore the collars around their throats that identified them as the sexual slaves of the beasts and chains that looped through nipple rings and clit ring. They glanced at her with little interest as Gaelen led her through and stepped into another corridor.

She looked back several times until a bend in the corridor blocked them from her view.

He had spoken the truth about the others, but she supposed she had already begun to realize that.

They were alive because Gaelen had cared for them as he had her, she realized abruptly, feeling a sick sensation knot in her stomach that she would have liked to think was revulsion but knew wasn't, even though she refused to examine the emotion and identify it. She had not been able to help but notice that the women had barely glanced at her. Their attention had been focused on Gaelen, and they had made no attempt to hide the hunger in their eyes.

It seemed to answer the questions that had rambled through her mind earlier. There were plenty of women quite close by that were eager to accommodate his needs.

She was tired, physically, mentally, and emotionally, when they came at last to a room virtually identical in every way to the others where she had stayed. He left her to 'rest', but she found she didn't particularly want to. When he'd gone, she got up from the bed and looked around the room, and then peered through the other openings. She discovered an area like those before for attending her personal needs and, to her pleased surprise, a small pool much like the ones before. Relieved that she would not be taken to the pool to bathe with the other women, she went back into the main room.

She had been lounging on the bed for some time, allowing her thoughts to wander at will when her gaze finally focused on the chest. Gaelen had still not returned, so she got up after a moment and moved to it, lifting the lid. The contents were neatly arranged, salves and potions in jars on one side, strips of linen on the other. Piled atop those somewhat more haphazardly, were harnesses, clips like those Gaelen had used on her and a number of objects that she had not seen before and had no idea of what purpose they might serve. There were several sets of manacles, as well, of varying sizes, either designed for wrists and ankles or simply for larger or smaller people.

There was also a flay and a whip. After staring at them for several moments, Lilith took another look at some of the harnesses, which she had dismissed, thinking they must be like the one that had been placed on her. Some of them differed rather drastically, however, in that once she had examined them she could see that the wearer would experience a high level of discomfort if not outright pain.

Returning everything to the chest, she frowned as she closed it.

Gaelen had said that the demons would feed off of her-- either her passion or pain and they did not particularly care which. A shiver skated along her spine. It seemed unavoidable that the contents of every chest were the same and equally impossible to dismiss that she might be very familiar with all of them if she had not listened to Gaelen.

Hearing footsteps from somewhere close by, she moved to the bed, resisting the temptation to run when she realized that he, if it was Gaelen, could hear her as well as she could hear him and running would indicate a sense of guilt.

It occurred to her as she settled on the edge of the bed, trying not to look as if she had been doing something she should not have, that she could not recall anything in a very long time that indicated that Gaelen listened to her thoughts. She knew he could. Many times, he had responded to things that she had thought as if she had voiced them aloud.

Had he closed his mind to her thoughts, shut himself completely away from her, she wondered? And, if so, why?

It was Gaelen she had heard. He entered the room with a tray of food even as she settled. He glanced toward her, met her gaze for a moment and then glanced toward the chest. Lilith looked away before he could turn to examine her face, turning and climbing further onto the bed.

He studied her for a moment and finally turned and set the tray on the small table and left.

Lilith frowned in confusion, and then irritation.

He might as well have said, *Feed yourself and do not bother me.*

From the time she had come, he had cuddled her and fed her himself, even before she had been so weak and battered and upset that she had not cared if she ate or not. She had been uncomfortable with his determined petting to begin with, but she had quickly grown accustomed to it, come to expect it. She had not realized until that moment, though, that the intimacy of that ritual was part of what had made her look upon Gaelen as her protector, a large part of what had made her feel that he held her in affection, that she was more to him that merely a vessel designed to entertain.

She tried to shrug it off, but she felt the pinch of rejection, felt dismay descend over her at the magnitude of the barrier he'd erected between them while she had been so focused inwardly that she had scarcely noticed him building it.

Slipping from the bed, she moved to the table, but the idea of sitting in the hard chair didn't especially appeal. Taking the tray, she moved back to the bed, setting it down and climbing up and bracing her back against the headboard. Folding her legs, she was about to settle the tray on her knees when an errant thought occurred to her.

Gaelen had left. He probably had no intention of sharing the food with her, but she thought it was possible that he would come back. He would certainly come back to retrieve it later.

If he did, she decided, perhaps she could see just how indifferent he had become to her.

It irritated her that she wanted to know, felt as if she *needed* to know. She should not have cared one way or the other, or perhaps she should have been relieved.

She thought it mostly just irritated her that he was being so stiff and cold when she was the injured party.

There seemed no getting around the fact that he could do cold shoulder far better than she could, which only irritated her more.

She was not really hungry. She should have been starving, for she had certainly worked very hard. She saw with a touch of dismay as she looked down at herself that she had grown noticeably thinner.

Maybe that was why he didn't look at her? She was not round and appealing enough to suit him anymore?

Feeling a mixture of anger and hurt when she decided that

must be it, she tore off a piece of the meat and ate it glumly. She had eaten a good portion of it and was contemplating going to get a drink of water when Gaelen returned. Immediately deciding against it when he sent an irritated glance in her direction, she plucked a grape instead. The fruit burst as she bit into it. Chilled droplets landed on her upper chest and slid down to form a glistening droplet on the tip of one breast.

She was on the point of wiping it away when she glanced at Gaelen and saw that he had grown perfectly still. His gaze was fixed on the droplet of juice. His stance and the look in his eyes sent a shaft of warmth through her. Slowly, as if he'd forgotten to do so before, he swallowed.

For several moments, Lilith's thoughts were so chaotic she couldn't think at all. As she noticed Gaelen emerge from his trance like state, however, she glanced down at the tray, frowning. Deciding to pretend she hadn't noticed either the juice or his fascination with its progress across her breast, she chose another grape.

Gaelen settled at the other end of the bed. His gaze, Lilith noticed, though, was not on the tray but on the tangle of red curls on her mound. Her chest seemed to seize, making it difficult to breathe at all normally. As casually as she could, she unfolded her legs, setting the sole of one foot against the mattress and moving the other leg slightly wider as she leaned over the tray and picked up a fat, juicy berry.

Leaning forward slightly, she bit into it. As she'd expected, juice spurted into her mouth, but also dripped, landing on her belly and weaving a trail downward until it disappeared into the hair on her mound.

Gaelen swallowed audibly. The sound was enough in itself to set Lilith's heart to racing a little faster. It took off like a runaway horse when he leaned forward abruptly, swiped the tray from the bed with one hand and grabbed her around the waist, hauling her across the space that separated them.

Chapter Six

Lilith had time for nothing more than a sharp intake of breath before his mouth closed with ravenous hunger over the tip of her breast. Gratified by the greedy tug of his mouth, dizzy with the rush of fiery sensation that went through her, Lilith uttered a small sound of need and braced her palms on his shoulders to steady herself, curling her fingers into the hard ridge of muscle along his shoulders. The sound, or her touch, seemed to incite him. He shuddered, suckling more feverishly at her flesh before it seemed he lost the little control left to him.

Shoving her back against the mattress almost as forcefully as he'd seized her, he moved over her on his hands and knees, licking and tugging and sucking at first one breast and then the other as if he would consume her. Lilith was writhing and moaning with need by the time he ceased to torment her tender breasts and moved lower, nipping and sucking at the skin of her lower chest and belly and sending flurries of goose flesh rampaging across her skin that made her achingly sensitive all over. He sat back on his heels when he had thoroughly explored her lower belly and the acutely sensitive skin of her inner thighs. Grasping her legs, he hooked her knees over his arms and burrowed his face against her nether lips, parting them with his tongue and laving the length of her cleft from the mouth of her sex to her bud of rapture.

A shaft of pleasure akin to pain stabbed through her as he caught the ring and tugged ring and flesh into his mouth. He teased that tiny bud of flesh as he had her nipples, tugging and sucking on it hungrily. Lilith bucked against him, wriggling, unable to remain still, groaning and gasping as she felt the rising tide of passion inside her, clawing at the linens of the bed.

He continued the exquisite torture until the building volcano of pent up passion exploded, spewing fire through her veins. She cried out at the force of the paroxysm that rolled over her, making her heart pound almost painfully against her chest wall. Darkness clouded her mind as she fought for breath in sharp gasps that skated the edge of screams.

She was still shuddering and gasping when he lifted his head away from her, caught her wrists and dragged her up until she was leaning limply against his chest. Grasping her buttocks, he lifted her upward, aligned the head of his cock with the mouth of her sex and drove her downwards again, impaling her on his hard shaft. Groaning at the pressure, she looped her arms limply around his neck, pressing her forehead to his chest as he lifted her slightly and pressed down on her again and again until she had sheathed him fully with her body.

He caught a fistful of her hair, dragging her head back and covering her mouth with aggressive possession, parting her lips and exploring the tender inner recesses in a restless quest to claim her completely that sent a fresh stab of exquisite pleasure through her. Wrapping his other arm around her hips, he pushed into her more deeply still, holding her tightly and grinding against her as if he could not get deeply enough inside of her.

She broke away from his mouth as he lifted her and pushed her down again, setting a jarring pace almost at once that bespoke driving, desperate need. The stroke of his hard shaft along her channel rekindled the embers of her passion. She caught fire, felt her body coiling to spring free of restraint again. It erupted as she felt his cock begin to spasm and spew his hot seed into her.

She leaned heavily, limply against him as the waves of rapture finally began to mellow into small aftershocks.

His broad palm glided along her back, stroking her for many moments, but then stopped as he came to himself. Shifting, he laid her back against the mattress and withdrew, settling on the edge of the bed, his back to her. Curling onto her side, Lilith watched him through half closed eyelids as he struggled to regain the normal rhythm of heart rate and breathing. Even as she reached to stroke his hard, muscular back, however, he rose and left.

Disappointment went through her but she found she was too exhausted to dwell on it for many moments before she drifted away in a haze of repletion.

* * * *

There was a comforting familiarity to the ritual of preparation Lilith woke to. As he had since the time he had brought her into the labyrinth, Gaelen woke her to attend her needs, fed her and took her to bathe her in the pool. When he returned to the room with her, he affixed the harness he had placed upon her when she had been summoned before.

A touch of doubt and uneasiness filtered through her though, as she watched his face when he bade her to lie upon the bed and pushed her legs apart. He seemed completely detached about the process as he grasped the flesh surrounding her sex and clamped it to the harness on either thigh. She couldn't quite put her finger on why that bothered her until he'd pulled her up to stand beside the bed and bound her wrists behind her.

It was the fact, she realized, that he did seem detached about it. He had pleasured himself with her, taken pleasure from her, but he seemed as distant as before. She realized as he covered her eyes with the blindfold that she had expected something else. She wasn't sure what, but she had expected some change in his attitude toward her, some unbending, some sign that she had broken through the barrier he'd built between them.

The tug on the chain pushed the anxiety to the back of her

mind. Her body immediately began to warm with anticipation and her mind focused at once on what was to come.

She stopped when the pulling ceased, standing still, waiting. Vaguely, she was aware of sounds and movements around her that denoted a large room filled with many demons, but she was used to that, too, and dismissed it from her mind as she felt hands on her, tugging and pushing until she bent over at the waist. The cheeks of her buttocks were spread wide and she felt pressure against her rectum, shoving that increased insistently until the muscles yielded and a hard rod entered her.

She panted, trying to relax her muscles to accommodate it as her shoulders were grasped and she was pushed upright again. Discomfort treaded the edge of pain as she settled onto the shaft as her legs were lifted upward. At the same time, a hand grasped her bound wrists and pulled down on her arms until her back arched, thrusting her breasts upward. Something was clamped to her wrist manacles to hold her.

Her legs were forced to bend and then her thighs spread wide, until the chill air brushed her sex, and then wider, until the moist nether lips parted. Still the pressure against her legs increased until she was panting with pain again. Relief surged through her when her legs were finally bound and the pressure eased slightly.

She was still struggling to catch her breath as the shaft in the nether area of her cleft began to pump and withdraw from her at a frantic pace. A mixture of pain and pleasure went through her, each vying for dominance. Pain had begun to take the upper hand when a hot mouth settled over her bud and began to gnaw and suck at it so vigorously that her focus instantly transferred from the thrusting shaft to the currents of pleasure radiating from her clit and into her belly.

Euphoria shot through her despite the discomfort,

building rapidly. She'd already begun to quake on the verge of release when she felt the shaft in her posterior convulse.

It was withdrawn as was the mouth that teased her, leaving her teetering on the edge but unable to complete the cycle and find her own release. She panted, struggling to deal with the abrupt departure of the stimuli her body craved.

Eagerness swept through her when she felt a tug at one breast. The sucking and nipping broke her fall, buoyed her upward again. The shaft, or another penetrated her, began to thrust at a frantic pace that she knew would swiftly bring him to culmination. She struggled to keep pace, focused on deriving as much pleasure as she could, but once again they outstripped her, took their pleasure and abandoned her to aching disappointment.

Confusion filled her as they approached her over and over, building the promise of release and each time leaving her panting, unfulfilled until she felt like weeping with frustration. After a time, when she was left wanting over and over, she ceased trying to find release and struggled against it.

It made no difference. It was as if they knew the very moment to stop and withhold what she craved.

By the time the restraints were removed and she was released, she was exhausted, throbbing and aching and so sensitive she could barely stand to be touched. She was allowed to rest and sleep for a time, to eat, to attend her needs, but it was hellish. She slept little, unable to rest for the twinges that kept sizzling and jolting through her.

It was far worse, she realized after a while, than anything they had done to her before. In the beginning she had had fear and dread dogging her each day, but each day that was quickly swept away by the pleasure they wrung from her over and over.

She had no fear now, but dread was already dogging her when she was prepared for the summons the following day.

Hope and anticipation warred with the dread, though, as they bound her again for their pleasure. It died a swift death. She had not been long upon the rack when she realized that she could look forward to more of the same as the previous day. As agonizing as it had been to be taken to culmination until she could scarcely catch her breath, until she screamed hoarsely with each successive explosion of rapture, being denied surcease was true torture. Occasionally, as the day wore on and her body reached overload, she would shudder in tiny shocks of release, but none strong enough, or enduring enough to give her real relief.

She was ready to fight Gaelen when he came to prepare her on the third day. His face grim, he subdued her without a good deal of effort and readied her anyway.

She was close to weeping with need as she was bound for offering again, but she realized finally what the lesson was.

They could give her pleasure, and they could withhold just as easily.

Gaelen did not come for her after the third torturous day. Instead, when she was weeping with exhaustion and the burning pain of unfulfilled need, she was released, settled onto a lumpy soft surface and abandoned. She lay as they left her, drifting in and out of awareness until the blindfold was removed. There was a tug at her arms and then the manacles were removed, as well.

Surprised and more than a little unnerved, she opened her eyes a fraction.

She was in a huge cavern she discovered. Mounds of pillows in bright colors were scattered about it. Around her she saw the demons, taking their pleasure from the women she had seen before in the great bath.

She should have been terrified at the monsters that surrounded her, for although most were man-like in general form, there was no mistaking them for men with their grotesque faces and horny or scaly hides--the snake like creatures, the two headed beasts, the mantakortus with his two pronged cock.

She should have been revolted to see them coupling openly, to watch the faces of the women contort in ecstasy and listen to their hoarse cries. Instead, she could think of nothing but her own aching need.

From time to time, she felt the gazes of one or another of the demons, but none approached her. After a time, when she noticed that the women would disappear for a little bit and return, she struggled to her feet and followed them, finding, as she'd suspected, a place to relieve herself and bathe.

And slowly it dawned upon her that the initiation had ended. She had become only one more of a harem of women who entertained the demons of the Labyrinth.

There were trays of food in the center of the great cavern when she returned. Many of the demons and a few of the women had gathered round to eat. Feeling weak and dizzy, she crossed the cavern and settled near a tray, more than half expecting to be pushed away when she tried to take some for herself.

Again, she was ignored and allowed to eat. When she had eaten her fill, she found a spot among the pillows, curled into a tight ball and drifted to sleep. She slept fitfully, though, her body still tormenting her with unquenched passion and aching even more when she was awakened by the sounds of coupling nearby and opened her eyes to watch, for the hunger in her instantly escalated to painful need.

Covering her head with a pillow, she drifted to sleep again. She was awakened by the glide of a hand along her thigh. Instantly, her heart hitched into high gear as she was rolled onto her back. The beast leaning near was an ugly brute, but she felt no fear, only the dread that he would take his pleasure and leave her aching for her own release.

She didn't even consider struggling, however, as he

placed his palms on her knees and pushed her thighs wide. Leaning down, he buried his face against her mound, opening a hot, hungry mouth over her sex. A shudder went through her as she felt her body surge to life. She gasped, moaned, reaching blindly for his head. Her arms were captured and pinned to the pillows as two more demons leaned over her and began to tug and suckle at her breasts. She wavered, fighting against the rising tide for many moments and then reaching a point where she lost the battle and began to struggle for release instead.

Disappointment filled her as the demon feeding on the tiny bud of pleasure abandoned it. Instead of withdrawing from her, however, he merely moved lower, covering the mouth of her sex with his mouth and sucking at the flesh there as he had the bud. Something hot, wet, and vaguely abrasive pushed into her passage and sent a shock of welcome sensation through her, making her belly clench. It delved deeper and deeper, undulating against the walls of her channel, rubbing against the walls as it lapped at her, gliding in and out. She bucked as the sensations escalated rapidly. He merely pressed harder against her knees, burrowed more tightly against her, sucking and licking ravenously at her body until the bliss crested and detonated in a fiery release. Ignoring the tremors quaking through her, he continued to suck and lap at her with his mouth and tongue until the tension coiled inside her again and a second culmination, harder than the first, washed through her and then a third.

She was scarcely even conscious when they moved away from her at last, drifting in a haze of sated bliss. She was not left long to rest, however. As if that had been a signal to the others, they drifted to her as it suited them, sated their hunger with her and took her to the heights of passion with them.

She realized, dimly, why she'd been blindfolded, for they were a fearsome looking lot and if they had not already trained her body to respond to them she wasn't at all certain she could have, or would have. None were beautiful like Gaelen, and some were truly terrible, but she found she didn't particularly care so long as they fulfilled her needs as they did theirs.

The two horned beasts were the most unnerving, but when the first approached her, pushed her onto her hands and knees and plowed his double shafted member into her, her body responded with excitement at the dual penetration.

Time passed in an endless round of carnal need and fulfillment. She slept, she ate, she bathed and took care of her other needs, and returned to the great cavern to repeat the process.

She had no idea how many days had passed when she became aware enough of her surroundings to notice that Gaelen had joined the gathering in the great cavern. Drawn by some force she was hardly aware of, she saw him on the other side of the ring of writhing bodies. He caught her gaze, held it as he mounted a woman with long, dark hair and began to pump into her furiously.

Heat coursed through her as she watched him, need, and something else she couldn't entirely identify--resentment, anger. She looked away when she saw his great, muscled body begin to tremble with release.

She could not tear her mind from him, though. Each time a demon took her and she looked up, she saw him watching her, sometimes as he coupled with another woman, sometimes merely watching.

He did not approach her, and she felt a mixture of fierce gladness and hurt that he didn't. Angry or not, she wanted him, and she began to imagine the mouths and tongues that fed her passions were his. She began to fantasize each time she felt a cock plowing and thrusting into her that it was Gaelen driving her to the brink of madness and then giving her surcease before her mind broke.

She thought she knew the moment he went away again,

but of course she couldn't be certain. She simply looked for him one day and saw that he was no longer among those in the great cavern.

For what she thought must be two days, perhaps three, he was absent and then he appeared one day leading a young woman by the chain he had used to guide her through the labyrinth each time she was summoned.

The demons and the other women stopped what they were doing and watched hungrily as the woman was bound for their pleasure. Lilith watched too, feeling uncomfortable heat coiling inside of her at the memory of her own trial.

She found that she was both fascinated and repelled by the woman's torment, recalling her own, and if she had not already completely understood what the sexual torment was about, it was crystal clear to her by the time the woman was finally released and left alone to hunger for the culmination that had been denied.

Her heart slammed against her chest wall and began to hammer painfully when she looked up and saw Gaelen heading directly toward her. In that instant, she completely dismissed the woman's pitiable state.

Without a word, he extended his hand to her. Mutely, she took it after the briefest of hesitations, allowing him to draw her to her feet and following him willingly as he led her from the great cavern and down a long, narrow, winding corridor.

They came to a smaller cavern, like those he had taken her to before. Expecting the same ritual as she'd grown accustomed to, she was surprised when he merely bade her sit on the bed and settled at the opposite end, studying her for some time before he at last spoke. "You crave the passion they have coaxed from your body over and over," he said slowly. "You hunger for it when it is withheld."

It wasn't a question. It was a statement of fact, and she knew nothing but the truth. She did crave it, with more hunger than the food she needed to sustain her, more than she thirsted for water when her body needed it.

"They have a new female to interest them. Do you wish to stay, knowing that your days will be filled as they have been? Or to go?"

Despite the fact that she had just acknowledged her need for the passion they coaxed from her, the decision was not difficult. The moment he offered release, she felt both the pain of loss and a desperate yearning to flee.

She didn't want to live as she had been living, not because she didn't crave it, and not because she still desired her freedom as desperately as before. She wanted to go because she realized the moment he said it that he was the only one she longed for. She didn't want to watch him with the others, even though she couldn't prevent the heated desire it engendered in her to watch him. She didn't want to feel the touch of the other beasts and yearn for him instead. "I want to go home," she said, keeping her voice even with an effort.

It startled him. She could see that it did, and that it touched off an avalanche of emotions in him. "Why?"

Lilith swallowed with an effort, casting around for something to say besides voicing the truth. "I miss my forest. I don't like the way I have changed. I don't want this gnawing craving inside me. I want to forget it and return to the life I had before."

His face grew taut with anger. "I could give you the gift of forgetfulness you ask, but the villagers will not have forgotten you. In their eyes, you are a threat to them, a witch, and they will not leave you in peace. If I take the memory of this to give you the peace you want, you will not know the danger they present to you."

Fear tugged at her, but she dismissed it. "Then I will go deeper into the forest where they can't find me," she said stubbornly, wondering abruptly if that was what her mother had asked for, forgetfulness. Mayhap she had not merely refused to talk about what had happened. Mayhap she simply did not know.

He sat up. "I will give you time to think about it."

"I don't want or need more time."

He settled to studying her again. This time, though, there was confusion and something else in his gaze, something she couldn't quite fathom.

He sat tensely for a time. Finally, as if he could not dismiss whatever it was that bothered him, he swallowed audibly. "Give to me what I want and I will do as you ask."

Lilith frowned in confusion. "What can I give to you? I have nothing to give."

"You have yourself to give. I want that."

Her confusion only deepened at that comment. He took, just as the others did, when he wanted. After a moment, though, she remembered what she had said to him before, remembered the hurt and anger she'd felt when she'd sought comfort from him and found passion instead. Reluctance settled over her. Her chest tightened painfully.

She found, though, that the appeal was far stronger than the reluctance.

Shifting on the mattress, she moved toward him. He sat up, his gaze eager and filled with wariness at the same time. His hands shook faintly as he turned and pulled her onto his lap so that she was facing him, astride his thighs.

He sucked in a harsh breath when she lifted her palms and settled them on his shoulders. His eyes slid half closed as she slipped her hands upward and cupped her palms on his cheeks, leaning close and brushing her lips lightly across his. Enthralled both by her own reaction and his, she lingered, nipping lightly at his lips, teasing them with her own until he released a harsh breath and opened his mouth over hers, delving inside the sensitive recess with his tongue. A shudder went through him when she entwined her tongue with his, stroked it, coaxing it into her mouth to suck on it.

His taste and scent engulfed her in a flash of heat.

Moisture pooled in her sex. She shifted closer still, luxuriating in the rioting sensations washing through her. His hands settled at her waist, clenching and unclenching, but he held himself still with an effort.

When she had explored his mouth thoroughly, she lifted her lips from his and explored his face with her lips and then his throat, the side of his neck, the swirls of his ear. The tremors running through him grew more pronounced as she explored his ear with her tongue, began to explore his body with her hands, gliding her hands lightly over his flesh. His chest expanded and contracted in deep, harsh breaths as she leaned down to explore the hard bulges and silky skin with her lips, as well.

Enthralled by his reaction, feeling her own desire rise in concert, she slipped backwards along his thighs and leaned down to take his engorged member into her mouth. He let out a sound that contained as much pain as pleasure as she sucked at his flesh, stroking her hands along his length. His hands squeezed her and released and finally withdrew as she cupped his testicles and began to massage them gently. He curled his fingers into the mattress, his body shaking more violently.

His trembling excited her, provoked a sense of power, and she began to move more quickly, striving to push him beyond control. He groaned, shifting beneath her touch as if he could not be still, grasping her shoulders and then releasing them again and curling his fingers into the mattress like claws.

The fiery tide of desire inside of her grew hotter as she teased him, coaxing his body nearer and nearer the boundary between extreme pleasure and release. Triumph filled her when she felt his cock jerk. He grasped her shoulders, as if he hardly knew what he was doing, struggling with the temptation to push her away and the driving need to find fulfillment. She ignored the slight push, working her hands and mouth over him more feverishly until she pushed him beyond the limits of his endurance and tasted his release, feeling her own body quake in a gentle release as he groaned hoarsely, sucking and stroking him until she had milked him of his seed.

He lay limply against the mattress when she lifted her head at last to look at him, his eyes closed, his chest heaving with each strained breath he dragged into his lungs. When his breath had ceased to labor and he lifted heavy lids to look at her, she said, "More?"

He swallowed thickly. "Yes."

She began as she had before, stroking her hands over his body, exploring his mouth and his flesh with her lips until he was groaning and shaking with need again. He jerked reflexively when she took his member into her mouth, groaning, his hips jerking as if he was fighting the urge to pump into her.

"Take me into your body," he gasped after a moment. "I want--I need to pump my seed into your womb."

She lifted her head, studied him a moment and finally came up on her knees to push his hard flesh into her passage, fighting her own need to impale herself on the turgid shaft and find a quick release. He groaned harshly as she moved over him with slow deliberation, drawing the pleasure out.

Abruptly, his restraint broke. Grasping her, he tipped her onto her back and rolled over her, pushing inside of her in almost the same motion. Grinding, into her so deeply she could feel his cock head butting against her womb with each desperate, unrestrained plunge, he brought her to crisis within moments. She cried out hoarsely as the spasms rippled through her in hard shock waves. Gritting his teeth, he drove faster still until his body convulsed, spilling his seed into her in a hot tide. He groaned, driving deeper still, grinding his pelvis against her to deposit his seed as deeply within her as he could.

Shuddering, weak in the aftermath, he caught the bulk of

his weight on his arms, dropping his head so that his cheek rested along hers. "I have planted my seed in your womb, little bird," he said harshly.

The words flickered through Lilith's mind but made little sense. In the time that she had dwelt in the labyrinth, many demons had bathed her womb with their seed.

"Only mine will grow. You were promised to me," he said harshly.

Lilith opened her eyes to look at him as he withdrew his flesh from hers and settled beside her.

Chapter Seven

Lilith studied Gaelen's face uncomprehendingly. "What?" she asked finally, beginning to feel doubt pierce the lingering euphoria.

"The lady of the forest, Gwyneth, she promised you to me long ago."

Lilith sat up and pulled away to look at him, trying to calm the chaos that had descended upon her the moment she heard him speak her mother's name. "You said you were not here when my mother came." A dreadful thought entered her mind. "You lay with my *mother*?"

Something flickered in his eyes. His skin darkened, but whether with guilt and discomfort, or anger at her tone she wasn't certain. "I did not."

She stared at him, abruptly scrambling from the bed. "You lied! You said you were not here."

A mixture of dismay, confusion, and anger flickered across his features. "I wanted her but I was a youngling then. She said that I was a child and would not give to me all that I wanted, not even as I grew and matured. She said that I was not meant for her, that you would come one day and I would know you because I would see her likeness in you."

Tears of rage filled Lilith's eyes. "You lie! She would not have promised me to you. I was not even conceived until long afterwards!"

He sat up. "She had the gift of sight. You know this," he growled.

She did know, but it made her feel no better to realize that her mother had not offered her, but had merely seen what fate had decreed for her. She might have been warned!

Why had her mother never said anything at all about the fate that awaited her, she wondered, feeling betrayed.

"I have waited for you," he said earnestly. "I was gentle and careful of you as she said I must be if I wanted you to give me what I yearned for. I gave you my child."

Lilith squeezed her eyes shut, allowing the tears to roll down her cheeks, feeling betrayed by the world. "Take it back!" she said angrily. "I do not want it and I do not want you! I only gave because you said you would free me, damn you!"

His expression went blank for several moments before anger blazed in his eyes. "*You* lie! I felt it in your touch! You gave from here," he growled, stabbing a finger at her chest above her heart.

Lilith slapped his hand away angrily. "You are a creature of the underworld! You do not even know how to feel any tender emotion! How would you know when others feel it?"

"I know," he growled implacably. "I learned gentleness from your mother. I learned to see it in her eyes."

"She did not teach you how to feel things you are not capable of feeling! She only managed to teach you to imitate the emotions!"

He paled, but after only a moment his face hardened. "Your womb would not have opened to me if you had felt nothing," he said harshly. "I *am* a creature of the underworld. I know this much, that we can not beget upon mortal women … and yet I have, because it was meant to be."

A flicker of hope went through her that he was right, that they couldn't, and he only thought that he had planted his seed because he wanted to believe it himself. "You said that you would set me free. I will find my own way if you do not. The others will not care. They have plenty of women to slake their thirst for flesh on."

He got up abruptly, towering over her. "Go then!" he

snarled furiously. "*I* do not care! The other females will slake my hunger, as well."

Too angry to consider that she had no idea how to find her way out of the labyrinth, Lilith turned and stalked out. She hesitated when she reached the great cavern, but finally headed toward the opening where she had seen Gaelen enter before.

A mantakortus caught her before she could reach the doorway. Grasping her hair and forcing her to bend forward, he penetrated her with his double pronged member before she could even fully grasp his intent. He released her almost as suddenly as he had grabbed her, so abruptly that Lilith sprawled onto the pillows strewn about the cave floor. Even as she struggled to roll over and get to her feet, a hand curled around her upper arm, snatching her up.

Gaelen's eyes were blazing with fury when she looked up at him.

Without a word, ignoring the gawking surprise of the other demons in the cavern that he'd interfered in the coupling, he marched her through the room and into the corridor. She began to struggle against him when she recovered from her own surprise. He ignored that, as well, dragging her behind him so quickly that she had to race to keep her feet beneath her. She was already short of breath by the time they entered the first of the small 'waiting' rooms where she had stayed before.

Her certainty that he had taken her there to punish her, however, vanished when he went through with barely a pause and out again into another passage. She was near to dropping with fatigue from the pace by the time they had winded their way along one passage after another, through cavern after cavern, some small, some tiny, some tremendous.

The light of day shining through the open mouth at the entrance to the labyrinth nearly blinded her when they came upon it, for she'd had nothing but the dull glow of torches to see by for many weeks. She shielded her eyes from the bright light as he scooped her into his arms, holding her tightly against his chest as he launched himself into the air.

Her stomach went weightless. Too unnerved to concern herself with her anger, she threw her arms around his neck, holding tightly. It seemed they flew for far longer than they needed to only to reach the mouth of the cavern high in the outer wall. Finally, Lilith felt them begin to descend. She did not loosen her grip, though, until she felt the jolt as Gaelen settled to the earth.

As he released her, allowing her feet to slide to the ground, Lilith looked around curiously and realized that they were deep in the forest. She recognized the stream nearby, for it led past her own cottage.

He caught her face between his palms, tipping her head back so that she was forced to look up at him. For several moments, he merely studied her. Finally, he slipped his hands upward until his palms cupped either side of her head and his golden eyes seemed to glow with an inner blaze. Mesmerized by the fire she saw in those golden depths, Lilith found she could not look away. Dizziness swept through her and then the darkness of nothingness.

* * * *

Lilith swam upward through the fog and surfaced, becoming aware of the sounds of the forest around her. Her head was pounding and she lifted a hand to it as she opened her eyes and sat up.

Crouched no more than three feet from her was a creature of the nether world, a Hawkin, she realized, as her gaze settled on the golden Hawk-like wings sprouting from his back. Unnerved by his unblinking gaze, she shifted away from him, afraid even to leap to her feet and try to run.

He made no attempt to stop her and some of the fear dissipated as she stared at him, frowning in confusion as a vague sense of recognition went through her. To her stunned surprise, his face contorted abruptly as if he was in terrible pain. His eyes grew glassy, as if moisture gathered in them. He squeezed his eyes closed, as if he could not bear to look at her, forcing the moisture to overflow and creating a shining rivulet along either pain contorted cheek.

Abruptly, he sprang to his feet and shot upward, flapping his great wings as he climbed skyward threading his way through the boughs of the trees. Still too stunned to do anything else, she watched until he disappeared above the tops of the trees, hidden at last from her view by the dense foliage.

Frowning, still confused, her head throbbing fit to split, she looked around, wondering how she'd come to be in the forest with no recollection of getting where she was. A shiver went through her as a breeze tickled over her and she looked down at herself, feeling a jolt of horror and even more confusion when she saw she was completely naked save for the obscene rings she discovered in her nipples, and lower, in her woman's place.

There was no sign of her clothing anywhere that she could see.

Had that *thing* raped her, she wondered? Was that why she was naked? Was that how she had come to be so far from her cottage with no memory of even getting here? Had he so terrorized her when he'd captured her that her mind simply had not been able to hold the memory?

He had not looked terrible, though, or even frightening. He had looked--hurt, so terribly wounded that she had ached to look at him.

She could not deal with that. She had no idea why she would feel empathy for his pain when she was in such distress herself, especially for a creature of the demon world, but she could not think about that now. She had herself to worry about.

Glancing around nervously to make certain there was no

one around to see her, she got up, found her bearings and began to race toward her cottage.

Relief filled her when she realized she was nearing the shelter she sought. She skidded to a halt, though, when she reached the clearing where her cottage sat, gazing around at her home in stunned disbelief. Her animals were gone, her garden flattened. The cottage had no door, no shutters. The wooden settle where she often sat on her porch to prepare the food from her garden had been broken into pieces. Fearing what she would find inside, she hesitated for many long moments and finally crossed her yard slowly to peer into the doorway.

Everything inside had been smashed and destroyed, everything that had remained, for it was virtually empty.

Too stunned even to feel anything at first, she backed away again and sank weakly to the stoop, staring blankly at the signs of destruction while it slowly seeped into her mind that everything that she had was gone or destroyed. Tears welled in her eyes and rolled down her cheeks. "Why?" she cried out with a mixture of pain and bewilderment, not even certain who she blamed, who she thought had done this. "Why did you do this to me?"

Curling up tightly in a ball, she dropped her cheek to her knees, wrapped her arms around her legs and sobbed brokenly for all the things lost to her; her mother's belongings, her own, and the curtains and coverlets and pillows her and her mother had made together--all the many things that had given her comfort in the lonely years since her mother had died.

* * * *

Gaelen was within sight of the mouth of the labyrinth before the pain fisting in his chest eased enough that he could drag in a deep breath, before his brain began to function again. He had meant to stay and watch over her until he knew that she would be all right, he remembered abruptly, feeling an inexplicable anxiety crush down on him as he recalled his concern that the villagers might try to harm her. Instead of heading directly toward the opening to the labyrinth, he cut a sharp circle in the sky, hovering for several moments and finally turned back the way he'd come.

It was not difficult to find her. He did not think he would have had great difficulty in any event, but he heard her weeping long before he saw her. Rage rushed over him at the sounds of hurt, at the protective way she had curled in upon herself. Once he had swept the area around her cottage with his keen gaze, seeking something or someone to rip to shreds, however, he saw that there was no sign of anyone else, no sign that any one had been anywhere near the place in many weeks.

Baffled, still struggling against both his own pain and his rage that she was hurt and he could not understand why, he settled finally on a broad bough above her, crouching to watch her and trying to fathom why she was weeping. She was not injured that he could see. It occurred to him that she might be afraid, but he could not believe that he had frightened her so much that that accounted for her wailing. She had looked at him with fear, true, and distrust and without recognition and *he* had felt pain as if she had stabbed him in the chest with a blade, so much pain that he still ached with it, but that would not explain hers.

Finally, reluctantly, he dragged his gaze from her and looked around in search of the answer. It was then that he realized everything was a shambles. There was no livestock anywhere to be seen, no neat fences. The cottage itself looked battered and broken. As many years as had passed since he had come to this place, he knew it had not looked like this before.

After a moment, he leapt from the bough, spreading his wings and gliding to the earth on the back side of the cottage and strode to the window to look in. Surprise and then fresh fury rushed through him as he took in the state of the cottage and understood at last why Lilith was so devastated.

The villagers had come after they had left her chained at the rock, he realized, and what they had not taken, they had destroyed.

It was a wonder they had not burned the cottage to the ground, but he supposed they had been too fearful the fire might follow the forest to the village and take their homes, as well.

The longer he listened to her sorrow, the angrier he became. Resolutely, he turned and left when he could bear it no longer, taking to the sky again and following the narrow ribbon of path that wound through the trees from Lilith's cottage to the village.

Most of the villagers were gathered near the center of the town when he reached it. Curbing the urge to descend at once in a rage, he circled slowly overhead while he considered the situation, trying to decide if he merely wanted to vent his fury upon them, or if it would be better to try to take back what they had stolen to soothe Lilith.

He thought it would make him feel better to destroy something, to release the pain and anger that felt as if it was choking him.

He had not wanted to let Lilith go. Mostly that had been because he could not bear to think of doing so, but he was afraid for her, too, because of what the villagers had done to her before. It had been harder still to remove her memories because he was a part of those memories and he had not wanted her to forget him. It had hurt when he had given Gwyneth the peace of forgetfulness, so much that he had never forgotten the pain even though he had been very young at the time. But even that had not been as bad as setting Lilith free.

Why had Gwyneth told him Lilith would be his if it was not so, he wondered angrily? She said that she had seen it, that he must remember the ways she had taught him so that he wouldn't harm his Lilith or frighten her and then she would give herself to him gladly. He could not understand what had gone wrong unless Gwyneth had lied to him.

He could not believe that, but he wasn't certain whether it was because he had been tricked by her sweetness and her gentle ways, or if he simply did not want to believe it.

As he studied the mortals below him, though, it occurred to him that, perhaps, Lilith had not been able to accept what he was. He did not look as mortals did. He had thought that it did not matter to her, for he had seen nothing in her eyes that told him she could not bear to look at him. There had been fear, naturally, because she was only mortal, after all, and he was certain he must be fearsome to such a fragile creature, but not revulsion, not terror.

Perhaps he had not really done anything wrong so much as he had simply not considered that his appearance might create a problem? If he appeared to her as they did, she would not be afraid and distrustful, and then she would accept him, he decided.

He had no sooner made the decision than doubt entered his mind. Would it be enough merely to look as they did? Or would she still say that he could not feel or understand the way mortals felt? And what if she did accept him as a mortal? He would have to live in the world of mortals, behave as a mortal, continue to look like a mortal.

It was not a pleasant thought, but he discovered very quickly that it did not matter greatly to him, not at the moment. As painful as it was to think that she looked at him now as if she had never known him, he *needed* to be near her. He did not think he could bear it if he could not, and he was certain that she would not allow him to come near her looking as he did.

His decision made, he ceased to circle above the village and dove for the earth. Hearing his approach, the villagers looked up, froze for several moments in their tracks and then began to scream and run in every direction. The temptation to avenge Lilith and vent his own spleen was nigh irresistible, but finally, reluctantly, he decided he would have to merely content himself with scaring them.

He had come for a reason and found another once he had arrived. He could not allow himself to be distracted by the hunger to kill and maim to purge the pain still churning in his gut.

After scanning them, he focused on the one man he decided was very near him in size. Diving for him, he used his wings to back stroke, breaking mid-air, and slammed his feet into the man's back. The man plowed the dirt with his face. Before he could get up again, Gaelen landed on top of him, pinning him to the ground.

Stepping off of the man, he bent down, grabbed him by the scruff of the neck and hauled him to his feet, sizing him up with his gaze. "What is this?" he demanded, plucking at the things the man wore to cover himself.

The man merely gaped at him, his eyes nearly bulging from their sockets. His mouth moved, but no words emerged. Frowning, Gaelen shook him. "Speak, or I will rip your tongue out and end the discussion now."

The man began to babble, but Gaelen could make no sense of anything coming out of his mouth. He shook the creature again and finally caught the man's face with one hand, speaking slowly. "What is this you cover yourself with?"

"C ... C ... C...."

"Bah!" Gaelen snarled, shaking the man again and then releasing him so suddenly that the man sprawled in the dirt once more. "I do not care what they are called. Bring some to me. And take care they are not full of holes or stinking of you. She would wretch at the foul scent you exude."

He discovered when he looked around that the rest of the villagers had vanished while he was occupied with the man. He smelled them though, smelled their terror. He knew they were close by, hiding. "The lady of the forest is mine," he bellowed so loudly that his voice echoed from building to building. "You took from her. You will gather all that you took and you will return it--before the sun sets or you will deeply regret it. Do not look at her again. Do not even *think* about offering her harm, for I will know your thoughts and you may be sure that you will beg me for death before I give it to you."

When he had finished speaking, he listened. He could hear the scurrying of feet, whispers, quiet weeping. Satisfied for the moment, he glanced around and spied a well nearby. Settling on the rim in a crouch, he studied the dirty village curiously while he waited, wondering why his Lilith would wish to live among such creatures when she would have been welcome to live among his kind, cared for, richly rewarded for all that she gave of herself. Why would she wish to toil as they did to survive? Why would she be willing to face their hatred and fear when she was accepted in the labyrinth?

Minutes passed. The sun moved. He got to his feet purposefully. As he did, a door burst open down the street drawing his gaze. A man and a woman, their arms loaded with baskets, shot from the cottage and began to run down the narrow track that led to Lilith's cottage. Gaelen settled back against the well feeling a sense of satisfaction as he heard other doors open and watched the villagers spill out of their cottages carrying the things they had stolen from his little bird.

The satisfaction did not last long. He did not at all care for the fact that he had sent the villagers stampeding toward Lilith and would not be there when they arrived. He'd begun to think he would have to track the man's scent to find the things he had sent for. Before the villagers had emptied the streets, however, the man reappeared carrying a bundle. He looked nearly as terrified as he had before, witless with it, and Gaelen had to wonder if the man had had enough mind about him to carry out the task. When he'd set the bundle down, however, whirled away to run and fell over his feet, plowing the dirt again, Gaelen strode to the bundle and untied it, examining the contents carefully and sniffing it.

He did not much care for the smell, but at least it was not the man's stench that permeated it. Bundling it up once more, he leapt upward, catching the air beneath his wings and soaring higher and higher until the villagers below him looked like ants racing along the trail to Lilith's cottage.

* * * *

Having cried herself out at last, Lilith mopped her face with her hands, pushed herself to her feet with an effort and went down to the brook to wash her face. She was still naked, and had nothing to dry her hands or face and the urge to burst into tears washed over her again. Sniffing them back, she trudged to the cottage and simply stood in the doorway for a while before she could gather the strength to move inside and begin to examine what was left.

Slightly heartened when she found a basket that was only a little misshapen and broken, she slipped the handle over her arm and dug through the debris. She found one of her bed linens beneath a pile of broken wood that had once been a stool. It was torn and not even the whole sheet at that. It looked as if two or three people had grabbed it and fought over it, ripping it into pieces. It was big enough, though, to tie around her waist and cover her lower body to her ankles. Feeling better still, she looked around more hopefully then and finally found another piece. It wasn't big enough to cover her as she would've liked, but she bound her breasts with it and felt decently covered, at least.

She'd gone back to sifting through the rubble when she heard a sound that made her freeze in dread and lift her head to listen more intently. She couldn't move for several moments after she first identified the sound as running feet, many feet. Finally, she managed to mentally kick herself into action and ran to the window. In the distance, along the track, she saw the villagers racing toward her cottage.

Her heart slammed into her ribcage so hard she thought for several moments she would simply pass out. Fear finally lent her wings, and she whirled and raced across the cottage, climbing out of one of the rear windows and fleeing into the forest to hide. Afraid to stop until she had put some distance between herself and the cottage, she finally reached the point where she could run no more and scrambled under some brush for concealment, fighting to bring her breathing under control so that she could listen for sounds of pursuit.

She could hear sounds coming from the direction of her cottage, but she could not tell what the sounds might indicate. The main thing, though, was that she could not hear anything to indicate that they had seen her and pursued. She'd just begun to think her heart might not beat itself to death when a crackle in the underbrush drew her attention and she turned to see a man coming through the forest, directly toward her.

Fear instantly washed over her all over again, but he moved unhurriedly and it finally dawned upon her that he must not be with the villagers. In fact, she did not recognize him at all.

He was a mountain of a man, she realized, and probably towered over most men. Long, inky black hair hung down around his face well past his shoulders. The lower half of his face was mostly concealed by a beard and mustache equally dark that contrasted sharply with the paleness of his skin.

He stopped when he reached the brush where she'd hidden, crouching down and peering at her through the limbs. "Why are you hiding?"

Lilith stared back at the man with a mixture of fear and embarrassment. She licked her lips, wondering if it would be safe to tell the truth. "Someone chased me," she said, finally settling on a partial truth.

He frowned, searching the forest around them with his keen eyes, which Lilith noticed were a strange golden color. She found it difficult to calculate his age. He was certainly a mature man for he had none of the look of growing into his body that very young men often had, but his face was not lined with age either.

It was a pleasant face, she decided, a very interesting face, handsome even, she thought, though that wasn't easy to tell either because of the beard and moustache. The long hair that flowed around his shoulders was as black as midnight, catching a bluish sheen like a crow's wing as he moved his head and the sunlight filtering through the trees struck it.

What sort of labor did the man do to make his living, she wondered, to be so pale? She could see his body was not fat, but taut and muscular as the body of one who labored long and hard.

A miner, perhaps?

"He is gone now."

Feeling awkward and silly, for she knew she could not have been hidden all that well when he had walked directly up to her, she struggled out of the brush and looked him over uneasily.

He was bigger even than she had thought, she realized, disconcerted by the fact that when he rose to his full height he dwarfed her and wondering if it would have been better to have run after all when he had crouched down and peered at her.

He frowned. "I do not mean you any harm. I came because I saw you running and I thought that you might need help."

"Oh," Lilith responded, feeling more embarrassed, but very little more at ease than before. He seemed unthreatening, but she was almost certain that he was a stranger to these parts and it was never wise to trust strangers. "That is so kind of you! I think, though, that I shall be just fine, now."

He grunted, glanced in the direction of her cottage and finally turned to look at her again. "I will walk with you to your cottage and make certain you are safe."

She didn't want him to, but she could think of no way to dissuade him if he was so inclined. His legs were long. She was swift when she needed to be, but she doubted that she could run fast enough to outrun him. It seemed better not to take the chance of arousing any hunting instincts he might have by trying to flee, especially when he was so close.

Mayhap, once he had walked her back to her cottage and was satisfied, he would go away again?

She would have preferred not to take him near her cottage, but then he had spoken as if he had already seen it and it seemed indisputable that he must know the villagers had been there since he had spoken of making certain she was safe.

Nodding, taking care to keep her distance from him, she struck off toward the cottage. She was in no particular hurry to return, not when there was a chance that some of the villagers might still be there.

She didn't know whether to be more relieved or more unnerved when she realized there were no sounds of activity near her cottage as they approached. She knew the villagers were a threat. She didn't know about the stranger, but she didn't feel particularly comforted by the idea that she would be completely alone with him so far from anyone.

"They are gone!" she said, allowing the relief she felt into her voice.

"They?"

Lilith glanced at him sharply. "He. I meant he--the one who chased me."

She saw the stranger's eyes were gleaming with amusement. "You do not lie well."

She reddened. "I don't know what you mean."

"It was not *a* man who sent you scurrying into the forest to hide. It was the villagers."

Lilith felt her color fluctuate several times while she tried to think up an explanation that didn't involve telling the man the villagers treated her with fear and distrust. Even though many of them had come to her over the years begging potions from her to cure their ills, the way they stared at her whenever she went into the village for needed supplies gave her the uneasy feeling that they believed that she was a witch.

She discovered as she looked around, though, searching her mind for something to say, that there was a large pile of debris near the front of her cottage that had not been there before.

Chapter Eight

Curious, Lilith forgot the uncomfortable question and crossed the yard to look at the pile, wondering if the villagers had been in the process of trying to set fire to the cottage and been frightened off, perhaps by one of the beasts from the forest?

She saw as she studied the debris, though, that it was not kindling piled at the door of her cottage. Gasping as she spied something familiar, she crouched down and pulled it from beneath a broken pot.

"This was my mother's," she murmured, pulling the faded blue gown from the pile and holding it up to study it. Feeling a surge of hopefulness, she folded the gown hurriedly and knelt down again, pulling out crockery, much of which was broken, and plates, linens, embroidered pillows that she had made, or her mother.

She was so busy searching the pile that she completely forgot about the stranger until he crouched down on the opposite side from her and lifted something up to study it curiously. "That was a pot I made when I was a little girl," she said, embarrassed by the poor craftsmanship that was obvious even though the vessel was broken now.

His face grew taut with anger. "You are crying because it is broken?"

She hadn't realized there were tears streaming down her cheeks. Wiping at them self-consciously, she shook her head. "Yes. No. I am just so very glad to have them back!"

He looked taken aback. "You are weeping because you are happy?" he asked doubtfully.

Lilith chuckled and then sobbed. "Yes, I suppose. I don't know."

She sat down abruptly, burying her face against the dress that had belonged to her mother. It had been stored in a chest with most of her mother's personal belongings since her mother had died, and it had *smelled* of her mother. Any time she had felt particularly lonely, or begun to miss her mother, she would take the things out and feel her mother's presence again.

Now it smelled only of dirt and unwashed body.

Someone had been wearing her mother's dress! They had brought it back, but they had taken something she could never get back.

She jumped when she felt his touch. She had been so sunk in her misery that she had not even noticed when he had gotten up and approached her.

Well, she had noticed, but she had thought when he got up that her weeping had driven him away.

The glide of his broad palm along her back was oddly soothing, though, so although she tensed, she did not pull away. She was surprised at how strong the temptation was to lean closer. Finally, because the urge was so overpowering, she straightened away from him.

"I will help you gather up what is not broken and carry it inside."

Lilith glanced at him in surprise. "Oh, no! I could not impose upon your good nature. You have been very kind, but I am sure you must have business of your own."

He studied her in silence for several moments, but she had the sense that he was sorting his own thoughts. "No."

She eyed him curiously. "No? You do not have business you need to attend to?"

"I am a stranger here."

She smiled up at him. "Yes, I know. Do you mean to say you have no place to stay?"

"I could stay here, and watch over you."

Lilith's jaw dropped. "That … that's so very kind of you! But … but I have no way to pay you."

He frowned at that. "It is not kind if you pay, is it?"

Lilith blushed, but she felt thoroughly confused. His eyes seemed to gleam with intelligence, but she began to wonder if perhaps the man was slow witted. He seemed almost child-like in his confusion about why she'd been upset. For that matter, he didn't seem to understand that it was simply not done for a man to be around a maiden when they were not wed. The villagers already despised her. If they discovered she had taken a man in to live with her, they would immediately assume the worst and they would certainly become very self-righteous about it.

Unreasonably so, since it was none of their affair one way or the other and it would not even have occurred to her to consider allowing him to stay with her if they had not done the things they had done.

He was a bull of a man, though, big enough to frighten any of them off if they should take the notion to come again.

"You have no home?" she asked tentatively.

He frowned as if the word was unfamiliar to him. "Cottage?" he asked, almost tentatively, as if he wasn't certain that it was the word he was seeking.

She blinked. "Family? A place to live, yes, but usually home means family."

He still looked confused. "You have family?"

She should not tell him she had no one, but then it was not like she could make him leave and if he hung around, he would see there was no one but her.

Poor man! He *must* be slow witted. If he had not spoken so clearly, she might almost have thought he was from some distant land that had very strange customs, for he did not seem to understand the way of her world at all. He looked as if he had managed to take very good care of himself, though--at least until now. And he was gentle, and seemed kind-hearted.

What did she care what the villagers thought of her? she

thought angrily. She had no reason to be ashamed. She did not intend to lie with him, but she needed help to set the place to rights, and it seemed to her that he had no where to go.

"You can stay," she said finally, "for I do need help, and I can at least find a place for you to sleep and food to eat, but you mustn't … uh…." She floundered as she gazed into his eyes, uncomfortable with the idea of telling him he must keep his hands to himself when she was the one who had allowed him to soothe her. Besides, if she was right and he was simple minded, he probably wouldn't understand.

He helped her sort through the things in her yard, making one pile of broken and not repairable, one pile of possibilities and then taking the things that were in fair shape into the cottage. Once she saw that he had the idea, she went into the cottage to sort the things inside and clean it up.

She had no shortage of firewood, she thought wryly as she piled her broken furniture near the hearth and started a fire. When she had it going, she took her iron kettle that she had found among the things the villagers had returned and went to the stream to clean it. Once she had scoured it thoroughly with the fine sand on the banks, she went to her wrecked garden and gathered what she could find that was still edible. That consisted of very little besides a few withered roots, but she didn't allow that to depress her spirits.

Pausing to watch the stranger for a moment, she finally approached him. "By what name are you called?"

Something flickered in his eyes, pain, she thought, but she could not imagine why it would hurt him to be asked his name and dismissed it.

"Gaelen."

She smiled up at him in genuine pleasure. "I like that. Gaelen. It is unusual, but it has a very nice sound," she said, realizing that she did like the sound of it. "I must go into the forest to gather some herbs and hopefully a hare to make stew if we are not to go hungry tonight. If you would, will you just try to get everything that is still good inside before dark?"

He nodded. "You will not be gone until dark?"

"I should be back long before that," she assured him, locating a basket that seemed fairly intact and heading off.

Poor man, she thought as she left. He was not at all handy. He could not have had a farm, she decided. She must have been right. He must have worked in a mine somewhere, for he had no skills at all that she could see for working around a place like hers.

She sighed. Beggars could not be choosers. She was not very skilled at such things as carpentry herself and the cottage would have to be repaired. She hoped that he was better at that than he was at cleaning and sorting, for it seemed to her as if he was only moving the piles about without making a great deal of progress.

* * * *

Gaelen watched Lilith uneasily as she disappeared into the forest, wondering if he should have insisted on going with her. He did not think the villagers would dare to come any where near her after he had told them that they would have him to deal with if they did, but there were beasts in the forest.

Turning to stare irritably at the piles of rubble in Lilith's yard, he wondered yet again why she bothered with it. He could not see that there was much left of any value, certainly nothing that could be used without some repair, at least.

And he had no notion how mortals did such things. He had watched her, but he could not see that she had done anything more than pick the things least damaged and piled the rest to one side for 'repair'.

The cottage was in more disrepair even than the things taken from it. There was nothing to close the gaping holes that let in light, but also annoying insects, and would make it easy for animals to climb in, both two legged and four legged.

Shrugging, he glanced in the direction that Lilith had disappeared and, when he saw that she could no longer see the cottage or the clearing around it, he summoned his powers and set about bringing order and neatness to the place. Satisfaction settled over him when he studied it a few minutes later. It looked as it had looked when he had come with Gwyneth. Lilith would be pleased, he decided.

He settled then to await Lilith's return, but discovered when he was no longer distracted by her, or the things she had set him to do, that he did not find the guise he had assumed the least bit comfortable. The hair itched, and the things the man had given him made to cover his body itched, as well, besides binding his body uncomfortably. His man root was not accustomed to being restricted in such a fashion and although he tried to reposition his sensitive flesh for comfort over and over there was simply none to be had with the twice damned bindings.

He got up after a time and paced the yard, realizing that Lilith had been gone for some time. Would it take her so long to find what she had said that she was going for, he wondered?

After several moments' indecision, he strode into the forest, discarded the man-things that were irritating his flesh and shifted back into his own form. He would not allow her to see him, he decided, but he wanted to make sure that she was all right.

She drew him to her by a strange sound. It was an oddly pleasant sound, but he could not recall ever hearing her make the sound before. He wasn't even certain of how she was making it. He could not see her lips moving.

Settling amongst the trees, he watched her for a while, relieved that she didn't seem to be in any danger, but curious as to exactly what it was that she was doing beyond making the strangely pleasant sounds that reminded him of bird song--except more rhythmically appealing. She searched the ground, frowning in concentration and stopping from time to time to pull a plant from the dirt and toss it into her basket. She would cease to make the sound for many moments, too, and then pick it up again.

Enthralled, he became incautious.

He knew the very moment she spotted him, for she went perfectly still, her eyes rounding. He held his breath, wondering whether to leave or stay where he was. After a moment, she seemed to come to a decision. Instead of turning to run, she began to walk directly toward him.

Disconcerted but strangely pleased, he settled in to wait to see what she would do.

She stopped several arm lengths away as if she needed the distance to feel safe from him. The thought made something clench painfully inside of him. She had not looked at him like that before he had taken her memory. She had looked at him as if she felt--safe.

"Are you … hurt?" she asked tentatively.

He felt something twist inside of him at the question. "I feel pain," he said, thoroughly confused by it, surprised that she seemed to know and feeling a mixture of relief and hopefulness that she would also know how to make it stop.

She hesitated, and then set the basket she'd been carrying down and moved a little closer, her gaze wandering over him. "I do not see a wound," she said finally.

He frowned. That was why he did not understand the pain himself. Even if he had been wounded, it would not have mattered. Such things healed very quickly. There was pain, regardless, when his flesh was pierced, but it left him when the wound closed. "I was not wounded," he said slowly.

Her frown cleared. "Perhaps it is something you ate?"

"I do not think so."

"Then, perhaps you are hungry?"

It was not the pain of an empty stomach. He knew that,

but he did feel hunger. He could not look at her without remembering what it felt like to bury himself deeply inside of her body and remembering made his body draw into painful tightness. She did not remember any of that, though, and he sensed that if he told her that was where he hurt she would flee.

Besides, the pain was higher more often than not. Almost as often, he mentally amended. He rubbed his chest.

"It hurts there?"

He nodded. To his surprise, she moved closer.

"You are not trying to trick me?" she asked, stopping again and looking at him suspiciously.

"No."

After studying him for several moments, she lifted a hand and placed it over his heart. Instantly, his heart began to race, sending blood surging through his body, making it difficult to breathe normally. A shudder went through him as she leaned toward him and placed her cheek against his chest.

She jumped back after a moment, her gaze dropping to his engorged cock. She stared at it for several moments as if it was a snake and then her head jerked upward. He tried to look impassive, but he did not feel the least so. He had to struggle very hard to keep from grabbing her and dragging her back.

"You are not hurt," she said accusingly, her voice shaky now.

He swallowed with an effort, but he didn't understand why it hurt when she looked at him that way and did not at other times and he didn't think that she would understand if he didn't. "I did not lie."

She studied him suspiciously for a moment. "Your heart is strong. You breathe rapidly, but I can not see that that would hurt your chest. There is nothing else there to hurt. When does it pain you?"

He swallowed, casting around in his mind for an answer

that would not involve telling her the entire truth. "It is the way … this mortal woman looks at me," he finally said lamely.

A look of surprise settled over her features. After a moment a mixture of sympathy and amusement entered her eyes. Her lips curled. "You are in love with a mortal woman?"

He was too stunned to say anything at first, but irritation surfaced after a moment. "I am not."

She looked unconvinced and more amused. "Then why does it pain you when she looks at you?"

"Because she does not remember me!"

The remark confirmed her suspicion as far as Lilith was concerned, but she frowned, wondering why the woman wouldn't remember such a creature, for he was certainly not forgettable. "But she should?"

"No. I took the memory from her because she did not want it."

"Oh!" The lingering amusement vanished and something completely unidentifiable washed over her, empathy for his pain, but admiration, she thought, too, and perhaps even a touch of envy. He must love the woman very much to be willing to do such a thing for her. She couldn't help but feel for him, and admire such generosity of heart. "You poor thing!"

He glared at her. He didn't particularly care to be called a poor thing. "I do not like this."

She smiled at him pityingly. "I am certain you do not."

"How do I make it stop?" he demanded.

She shrugged. "Unless you can make yourself forget, I don't suppose you can."

His frustration magnified. "I do not think I want to forget," he said finally, wondering why he did not when, if it was as she said, forgetting would give him peace from what was often nearly intolerable pain.

"In time, it will not hurt so much if you will not go to see her," she said gently. "The memory will fade on its own. If you loved her enough to take the memories and give her peace, then she did not appreciate you as she should have and it is far better to stay away."

He swallowed, his face twisting with pain. "I do not think I can stay away. I fear someone will hurt her if I do not guard her."

Deja'vu swept over Lilith at that remark. Disoriented by the strange sense of having done this before, been here before with the strange creature, dizziness assailed her for a moment. She frowned. "You are … most noble and good hearted. I confess I had not believed…." She broke off. "That is to say, I do not know anything about Hawkins at all. That is what you are?"

He looked pained by the question. "Yes."

He looked so hurt and miserable, she felt the urge to cuddle him and offer comfort. She supposed it was because she always had so much trouble resisting anyone or anything in pain. Something inside of her compelled her to try to comfort, even when she knew that there was danger in doing so. She stepped away instead. "I wish I could do something to take your pain away, but I'm afraid I can not."

He studied her for several moments, realizing abruptly what he needed. "Teach me how to make her love me."

"Oh! My! You really do not understand mortals at all, do you?"

"It can not be done?" he demanded with a mixture of anger and dismay.

She grimaced. "I am not at all certain I could help you. I have never been in love myself, you see. And then, too, I think it is something that simply happens between two … uh … people."

His eyes sharpened. "You are saying a mortal woman could not love one of my kind?" he demanded harshly. "Why? You said that what I felt for her was love. If this is true, when this is something that I have never known to happen to any others from the nether world, then why would she not be able to love me in return?"

She reddened. "I suppose it *is* possible, but … the thing is, you see, love is nature's way of insuring the renewal of life. It is part of mating, and like must mate with like in order to do that."

"I gave her my child," he said harshly. "It can not be that."

Excruciatingly uncomfortable with the direction the conversation had taken, Lilith looked around uneasily. "Oh! Well, this is very complicated. I think I must go now."

He looked so miserable when she backed away from him that her heart failed her. She could not think of any way to help him, and yet she could not bring herself *not* to try. If she could do nothing more than distract him from his grief she felt like she had to make the effort. "I will think about it," she promised. "Perhaps something will come to mind, some way that I can help you, but I must go now and find something for my cook pot or I will have nothing to eat tonight."

He did not follow her, to her relief, and when she glanced back a little later, having gathered what she could to fill her pot, he was gone. The snare she had set in hopes of capturing meat for her stew was untouched she discovered when she went back to check on it. Sighing dejectedly, she finally dismissed it. Soup was not going to be very filling, especially for a man the size of Gaelen, but it could not be helped.

Distracted as she was by her encounter with the demon and her pathetic gathering for her cook pot, she was half way across her yard before it dawned upon her that nothing looked as it should. She dropped her basket from suddenly nerveless fingers then, halting abruptly in her tracks. Speechless, disbelieving, she stared at the cottage and yard, expecting to find after a moment that her mind was playing tricks on her in the gathering gloom of the late afternoon. Gone was any sign of the destruction she knew the villagers had wreaked upon her place. Save for the fact that none of her livestock milled about the yard, everything was as she remembered before the attack---long before the attack. For she saw things that she could not recall seeing since she was a child; her garden where it had been before she had cleared an area for a new garden; the coop that had once housed her and her mother's birds, but that had fallen down many years ago.

Finally, remembering the food she'd gathered, she knelt to retrieve the basket and pick up what had fallen out. She saw, when she looked again, that the view was unchanged-- or rather drastically changed from when she had left it only a little earlier. The yard and the cottage looked as it had before it had been ransacked and everything trampled over.

Even her garden looked as it had before, lush with growing things--except in the wrong place.

Wondering if her mind had snapped, she crossed the yard and opened the door to the cottage, peering inside. Gaelen was kneeling at the hearth, placing a rack of hares over the dancing flames.

The inside of the cottage looked the same as she remembered *before* it had been destroyed by the villagers.

Gaelen looked up at her entrance, studied her stunned expression for several moments, and then, looking somewhat conscience stricken, looked away again, studying the flames on the hearth.

"You have … gotten so much done!" Lilith said a little faintly. "I must have been gone far longer than I thought."

"I thought it best to start inside since we would need a place to sleep tonight."

"But…." When she turned and looked at the yard, Lilith saw it as it had been before she had gone into the woods to look for food. Another shock wave washed over her, leaving her feeling dizzy and ill. Her mind *had* snapped! There was no other explanation. She had been so devastated at what they had done she had simply wished everything back as it had been and begun to believe she saw it that way. "I do not feel at all well."

Gaelen surged to his feet and took the basket from her limp hand. She gasped in surprise and a touch of alarm as he swept her into his arms and carried her across the cottage to the little room where she slept, settling her on the bed--which had been repaired just as everything else had.

Or maybe, she thought, nothing had been damaged--except, possibly, her mind?

Something had happened to her in the woods. She had avoided even trying to sort through the why and how she'd come to find herself in the woods, naked, and with no memory of having gotten there. But she simply could not remember, and she had to wonder if whatever it was had deranged her mind completely. Gaelen *could* have set the cottage to rights, but he had not had time to repair the furnishings that she had thought were destroyed.

"Rest," Gaelen said after studying her worriedly for several moments. "I will cook."

"Oh no! I should do that. You have worked so hard. You must be tired."

"I am not tired. I will cook."

She settled back, feeling guilty, but vaguely ill, too. Her head was swimming. She thought, perhaps, that she had overindulged herself with her self pity, weeping and wailing over every little thing until she had further unsettled her mind. Maybe it would be best if she did rest? And then on the morrow, if she was still not as she should be, she would find herbs to steady her nerves.

That must be it, she decided, shock and hysteria.

Finding that she was worn out from everything that had happened, she drowsed. Gaelen woke her when he came into her room a little later. She saw that he had brought food. Disconcerted that he had come into her room, twice, she looked at him uncomfortably, trying to think of a kind way to tell him that he was not to take such liberties. She was fully clothed, but nevertheless, not properly dressed and....

He settled the platter he carried on the bed and plopped down beside her.

Lilith stared at him in stunned surprise as he tore off a bite of food and lifted it to her lips. "Gae...."

He shoved it into her mouth when she opened it. Blinking in surprise, she chewed the piece of meat instinctively, swallowing. "You shou...."

She frowned at him when, again, the moment she opened her mouth, he shoved food into it.

The next time, she grabbed his wrist. "I can feed myself," she said, trying not to sound too mean about it.

"I enjoy feeding you, little bird."

Lilith glanced at him sharply, feeling that same odd sense of familiarity that she'd felt before in the forest with the Hawkin, as if she had done this, or something very like it, before, which was very strange when she had never set eyes on Gaelen before she had met him in the woods.

"Why did you call me that?" she asked curiously.

Something flickered in his eyes. He looked down at the food, frowning, as if he was trying to decide what he wanted. "You are tiny and quick, bright eyed, and also soft and white with brilliant locks of hair." He swallowed audibly. "And you only sing when you are free."

Flattered but also embarrassed, Lilith couldn't think of anything to say for several moments. "I am not tiny," she said finally. "It only seems so to you because you are so very big. I expect everyone seems tiny to you."

He shrugged. "I do not notice everyone."

Lilith was so disordered she didn't even think to object when he lifted another bite of food to her mouth. She took it, nipping at the tips of his fingers as she did so.

Embarrassed all over again, she reddened, but a strange warmth spread into her belly when she met his gaze that seemed to have very little to do with that kind of discomfiture. "I am so sorry! I didn't mean to bite you."

The gleam in his eyes grew more distinct. A faint smile curled his lips. "I do not mind your nibbling, little bird. If you are hungry…."

Chapter Nine

Abruptly an image, conjured by his comments, rose in Lilith's mind that was so carnal it sent a flash of heat sizzling through her. Her belly clenched, moist warmth filling her woman's place. She ducked her head, wondering what in the world had come over her to think such thoughts. She had never even kissed a man on the lips! Why would she be thinking about kissing ... nibbling on ... the rest of his body?

She was far more disconcerted when she realized it was the Hawkin's body that filled her mind's eye. It was certainly not Gaelen, for she had not even seen him without his shirt. She knew he was strong, and very muscular, but she doubted very much that his body looked like the Hawkin's.

He broke off at her expression, returning his gaze to the tray.

It was desire, she realized, and still wondered at it. Despite her inexperience, she was hardly ignorant of such things, but she could not recall that she had ever equated it to herself. She could not recall ever having felt any hunger of the flesh at all, let alone anything as powerful as the images in her mind had produced.

"Thank you, but I am not very hungry," she mumbled uncomfortably after a moment.

He glanced at her. "I will leave it. Perhaps your appetite will return."

He hadn't eaten much himself and she knew the tray contained all of the food that he'd prepared. "You eat," she urged him. "You have worked hard. You must be hungry."

"Only if you will eat."

She stared at him a moment, vaguely irritated with his insistence, but finally chuckled. "All right. But I will feed myself so that you can eat. And you can tell me about where you come from."

Gaelen choked on the bite of food he had just taken and sent her an uneasy glance, keenly aware that he had not considered that it might be necessary to concoct a story to explain his presence. What made it worse was that he had no notion of how men lived, what they did with their days, or even more than a vague idea of their social structure. She had mentioned family, home, and work, but he could see that she did not think that he knew anything about the workings of a place such as hers so he doubted she would believe him if he tried to tell her anything of that sort and unfortunately his experience with her was the limit of his experience outside the nether world. "I will get water," he said in a strangled voice and got up abruptly and left.

Lilith watched him worriedly, but finally decided that he could not be strangling or he would not have been able to speak.

When she had waited for what seemed a very long while, she got up and went to look for him, but although she called to him, she heard no response. After debating the matter for several moments, she left the cottage and headed toward the brook. Reaching the place where she usually drew her water without having seen him, she called again.

A splash further along the brook drew her attention. "Gaelen?"

"Yes."

"I was worried when you did not come back."

The splashing drew nearer. "I decided to bathe."

Since he said that just as he stepped within view of her Lilith hardly thought it was necessary. As dark as it was, he was pale skinned and the moonlight left little to the imagination. Lilith clapped a hand over her face, whirling away, but it did not help much. The image was burned upon her mind's eye. "Merciful heavens! I beg your pardon."

She beat a hasty retreat back to the cottage, scampered into her room and slammed the door. Spying the remains of their meal, she dashed to the tray and rushed into the main room of the cabin with it, setting it on the hearth before she retreated once more, closing her door and barring it with the small table that usually sat beside her bed.

A hysterical giggle of shock escaped her as she clambered into her bed and drew the covers over her head. She covered her mouth with her hand and then her pillow, trying to listen for his return.

She did not know what to think of the man beyond the fact that he was the strangest mortal she had ever known. One moment, he seemed not to know the simplest of things and she was certain he must be slow witted and the next he spoke or behaved perfectly normally, even cleverly.

She decided when time passed and he did not return that she had embarrassed him as much as she had embarrassed herself. Or perhaps he thought he had frightened her and was wary of returning for that reason?

She fell asleep worrying over it.

The sound of chopping wood woke her the following morning when the light had barely begun to spill into the room. She lay listening to it for some time trying to place the sound and then wondering at it when she realized that it was indeed someone chopping wood.

Memory of the night before flooded back abruptly and Lilith felt her face heat. It was Gaelen, the stranger she had welcomed to stay with her, though his body was certainly not unknown to her anymore. With great reluctance, she got up and headed out of the cottage toward the brook. Gaelen paused as she passed him. She nodded and kept going.

When she'd attended her needs and bathed, she felt a little more able to face him.

She saw when she reached the clearing again that he was chopping posts. She thought that was what he was doing. The logs he was cutting were far too long to fit into the fireplace. "Have you broken your fast?"

The distraction made him miss the log he was chopping at and Lilith felt her heart leap into her throat. Fortunately, he managed to miss his leg. Unnerved by the incident, she hurried back into the cottage without awaiting a reply, wondering if she should even allow him to chop wood since he did not seem particularly skilled at it.

There was food left from the night before, she saw, and she stirred up the coals in the hearth, fed more wood into the glowing embers and heated the food. She was setting out chipped plates and crockery when Gaelen came in. "We have no bread," she announced. "Nor anything to make more with, I'm sorry to say. I think I must see if I can find something to trade and go into the village, for we must have bread."

"No."

Lilith glanced at him in surprise.

"I will go."

She frowned, uneasy at the idea of sending him to trade for her. "They do not trust strangers. I would rather go myself than risk that you will run into trouble."

He sent her a speculative glance. "I am not concerned."

She smiled. "I am sure you are not, and I do not doubt that you are capable of taking care of yourself, but I would not want trouble on my account."

"I will eat the bread also."

She settled on the opposite side of the table from him, realizing that the longer she argued the matter with him the more determined he would probably be to go himself. "You will try not to get into trouble, though?"

He seemed to consider that for several moments and finally shrugged. "Yes."

She was not greatly reassured, but she left it at that. When they'd finished eating, she got up to clean and search for something to trade. There was no livestock to use in trade, but she remembered that the miller's wife liked pretty things and dug around in her mother's chest until she had found a gown she was willing to part with.

"That was your mother's."

Lilith glanced at him in surprise. "How did you know that?"

He looked disconcerted. "That is your mother's chest."

"Oh. Yes, and I am reluctant to part with it but Mother would have thought that I was daft to consider keeping something I can not use when I--we, need the food."

Bundling it carefully, she explained how much she thought he should be able to get for it and sent him along his way, watching worriedly until he was out of sight. She decided, though, once she had examined the pile of wood that he had cut that he could not be in any more danger from the villagers than he was from himself.

She decided to hide the ax before he managed to hack his foot off with it. She did not want to embarrass him, and she was afraid that she would not be able to express her concerns over him injuring himself without wounding his male pride. Hiding the ax seemed the most prudent thing to do.

After surveying the garden and the shed, she was forced to admit that they would have to work very hard--assuming that Gaelen did stay a while--or they would not have enough food to keep body and soul together. Her first garden had been ruined, but it was still early enough in the year, she thought, that she could replant it. She spent the morning gathering what she could from the demolished garden and storing it and then reworked the rows and planted what seed she had left.

It would not be a very large crop, she thought wryly, rubbing her back absently when she had finished, and if Gaelen did stay they would need more food even than she usually grew for herself. Glancing at the sky, she saw that the sun was almost directly overhead. Her stomach rumbled with hunger at just about the time she noted the noon hour, but she was hot and sweaty from working the garden.

After a brief mental debate, she decided that it would be safe enough to go down to the brook herself and bathe. Gaelen was not likely to return for several hours yet. Stoking the fire again when she went inside, she tossed what was left of the food into her cook pot to make a stew and settled it where it would cook slowly and then gathered what she would need for a bath and headed to the brook.

The water was icy. Mostly she was glad it was, because there was an endless supply of cool water to drink and the water helped to preserve some of her foodstuffs, but it was not a pleasant place to bathe and she always found herself dreading the first few moments until she became accustomed to the chill.

Today was no different, but she was not confident enough in her guess of the time when Gaelen would return to want to linger anyway. Scrubbing herself quickly with the soap she'd brought, she rinsed off as quickly and stepped from the brook, shivering, breathless from the chill.

The Hawkin, she discovered, had settled on the fallen log where she'd left her change of dress. She came to a jolting halt. It wasn't until his gaze moved over her with patent, heated interest, though, that she recovered enough from her surprise to cover herself. She glared at him. "What are you doing here?"

He sat up. "I came to talk."

She'd forgotten she had promised him that she would try to think of a way to help him with his lady love. "I am not dressed!"

"No."

"You must go away until I am dressed!" she said sharply when he made no attempt to leave.

His brows rose. "It bothers you for me to see you?" he

asked curiously.

"Of course it bothers me," she snapped.

"Why? You are beautiful to my eyes."

Her jaw dropped. She blinked rapidly for several moments, trying to think of an answer. "Because."

He got up slowly, lifting her gown and moving toward her. She would have retreated except that she could not seem to command her feet to move in any direction.

He stopped less than an arm's length away and held out the dress. When Lilith reached for it, he reached for her, flicking one of the rings in her breasts with his finger. A wave of heat washed through her dizzyingly. "Why do you wear this?"

Snatching the dress from him, she turned her back to him and shimmied into it. "I do not know. I do not remember how it came to be there, but I could not take it out," she muttered shakily. There had been a thin chain, as well, strung through the rings, and through another ring lower, in her woman's place, connected at each end with a collar. She had no recollection at all of having gotten any of it, but she had found that she was reluctant to speculate on it. The rings had simply been there where before they had not.

She had wakened naked in the woods with no recollection of having gotten there, her home destroyed. It took no great leap to imagine that the villagers who must have destroyed the cottage had done that to her also, but she could not think of a reason for it and she did not want to remember how, or why, or when they had done it to her.

Feeling better once she was covered, she turned an irritated glance upon the Hawkin. "It is not at all gentlemanly to stare at a lady in her bath," she muttered.

He tilted his head, studying her with amusement. "I am not a gentleman. I am a Hawkin."

That seemed inarguable. She sent him a resentful glance. "If you are in love with a mortal woman, you should know that … that she would not like for you to stare at another that way. You should be devoted to her alone."

His eyes narrowed speculatively. "This is the way of mortals?"

Lilith had already drawn breath to assure him that that was exactly the case, but she knew that was not true. Women generally devoted themselves, men rarely did. "If she knew she would not like it," she said finally.

"Why?"

Lilith pursed her lips in irritation. "Because."

"I do not understand this 'because'. What is the meaning?"

Lilith huffed irritably. "I am only saying that, if it was I, I would not like it and I think most ladies would feel the same."

When she glanced at him again, she saw that he was looking thoughtful.

"Because then she would doubt that you loved her and fear that you would leave her for another who was prettier."

To Lilith's relief, he moved back to the log and settled on it. She would have been *more* relieved if he had not been naked. She had been too wrapped up in her fear when she had first seen him to be really aware of it and too focused on her sympathy for him the day before to notice--much. At least, she had been so wrapped up in her empathy that she had managed to mostly ignore it, but she could not help but be acutely aware now. She didn't know if that was because of the thoughts that had so disturbed her the night before, because she had felt so vulnerable when she had found him watching her, or because he had breached a barrier when he had touched the ring in her breast. Whatever the case, it made her feel uncomfortably warm to look at him, unnervingly aware of her own sexuality no matter how carefully she tried to keep her gaze upon his face.

"You said that you would teach me the way to make her love me."

Lilith rubbed her temple. "I said that I would try. I do not know her."

He tilted his head. "You know you. Tell me what would please you."

There was a huskiness to his voice that sent quivers of heightened awareness through her when she had only begun to relax, distracted by his questions. She swallowed with an effort. The images that had assaulted her the night before when she'd come upon Gaelen bathing descended upon her like a thunderclap, so vividly that she felt a flash of scorching heat. "I do not know," she whispered finally. "I have never been wooed."

Confusion flickered in his eyes. "This woo is to make love?"

Lilith reddened to the roots of her hair. She cleared her throat. "It means something different when you say it like that."

He looked more confused. "The woo?"

Lilith bit back a smile. "The wooing is the courtship, the mating dance. First you see, and then if you are attracted, you want and you try to attract their interest--by being pleasant, and clever, and doing things to please."

"So, the wooing is to make love?"

"Something like that," Lilith muttered, deciding that it hardly mattered that he did not seem to grasp the distinction between making love, and making someone fall in love, since doing so led to the former. She did not feel up to explaining the difference in any case, particularly since she was convinced that he knew far more about the culmination of love than she did. He had said that he had given his lady love his child.

Not that she was certain that she believed that--that he would know. Men didn't know. Women didn't even know at first. She knew that there must be a vast difference between the beings of earth and those of the nether world, but she couldn't imagine having control of such a thing as conception.

He got off of the log and approached her again. This time Lilith took a step back. He stopped, studying her for several moments. "It is this form, yes?"

Lilith blinked, all at sea. "What?"

"You said that she must see me as pleasing. She is pleasing to my eyes, so beautiful to me that I can not breathe when I am near her and I am so slow witted I can not think. She would feel the same if I was pleasing to her eyes, yes?"

Lilith stared at him a little helplessly. To save her life, she could not resist looking at him when he impelled her to do so by his anxious question. At first, her impressions created so much chaos in her mind that everything seemed a great blur. When her perception finally sharpened, however, she discovered her gaze was riveted to his man root. She hadn't realized *that* was what a man looked like.

But perhaps it wasn't?

She could not recall what Gaelen's man root had looked like. She had been too stunned by his nakedness to remember more than bare skin, a lot of bare skin.

She cleared her throat, dragging her gaze upward with an effort until she met his gaze once more. "Does she see you like that?" she asked the first question that popped into her mind.

He looked offended. "We do not wear c--c--c."

Lilith stared at him blankly. "C--c--c?"

He plucked at her sleeve. "Man things."

Her mind went instantly to his man thing. She looked down at it again before she thought better of it. Like the rest of him, it was massive and intimidating. She meditated over it for many moments before she could draw her mind from it. It dawned on her when she looked up at his face again that he had plucked at her sleeve. "Clothes?"

He thought it over. "He did not say clothes. I recall very clearly. C--c--c."

"He?"

He brushed that aside. "Clothes would please her? It is not the face that fails to appeal? It is not the color of the flesh? Not the wings? Not because I have no locks such as yours?"

Lilith rubbed her temples, wondering if there was any way to say, without offending him, that it was all of him together that was appealing, but also so different that it was unnerving. "I do not even know your name," she said finally.

"Gaelen," he responded promptly.

Lilith gaped at him, stunned. "Gaelen?"

Wariness entered his eyes. "Yes."

"That is--so very strange!"

He looked offended again, but there was something else in his eyes, too, something she couldn't quite interpret.

"I did not mean the name was strange. It is a very nice name. It is only very strange that the man who helps me is named Gaelen, as well."

He looked disconcerted. After a moment, he looked away. "This man appeals to you?"

Her jaw went slack. "I--uh--I don't know. What I mean to say is he is very sweet."

"Sweet?"

"Kind, helpful."

"But does he please your eyes?"

"Oh!" Lilith said on a sudden thought, feeling blood pulse in her face at his question even as it hit her that Gaelen was liable to return at any moment and find her with the Hawkin. "He will be back soon. I must go now!"

Whirling abruptly, she charged back up the path that led to the cottage, torn between relief that she had suddenly remembered something that was a very good excuse to depart and the uneasy feeling that she had been extremely rude when she had left. Her dinner was sizzling and popping in the kettle when she burst into the cottage. The smell of scorched food permeated the air. Muttering irritably beneath her breath she grabbed a handful of her skirts to protect her hand from the heat and removed the kettle.

It was just as well, she thought, that she had lost her appetite for there was very little left in the pot that was not blackened and even the food that wasn't burned tasted dreadful.

It was almost sunset before Gaelen returned from town. Lilith had grown so anxious that she'd begun to contemplate going after him. It flickered through her mind to wonder if he had simply taken what she had given him for trade, traded for what he needed and kept going, but she found she could not accept it. He had been nothing but kind and gentle and helpful since he had found her hiding in the woods. She could not believe that he had broken her trust in such a way.

She was standing near the track that led to the village watching for him when he first came within view. Relief and gladness poured through her as she searched him for any sign that he had been embroiled in a fight, any sign that he was hurt. It was for that reason that she did not at first really notice the barrow that he was pushing.

Curious when she finally did notice the thing was filled almost to overflowing, she hurried down to meet him.

"You did not have trouble?" she asked anxiously when she neared him.

"Nay."

Joining him, she turned and fell into step beside him. "What is all this?"

"Supplies."

Her eyes widened. "You got all of this for my mother's gown?"

He slid a speculative glance in her direction. "Aye."

She frowned.

"And other things," he added when he saw that she looked skeptical.

"What other things?"

He frowned pensively.

"Gaelen! You did not … take, did you?"

He sent her a wary glance. "Nay."

She stopped him as he reached her yard, placing a hand along one cheek to make him look at her. "Then how did you get so much?"

Something flickered in his eyes. "I took a boar, as well."

Surprised again, she allowed her hand to drop. "A boar?" she echoed. "You killed a boar on the way to the village? With what?"

He shrugged. "My hands. I broke his neck."

Lilith's eyes widened. Feeling a jolt of uneasiness, she checked him once more for any sign of injury. "How?"

"He was caught in a mire."

"Oh, Gaelen! That was so … dangerous! You could have been hurt badly."

"I was not."

"But you could have been!" she said almost angrily, feeling perilously close to tears. "You must never do anything like that again! Promise me!"

He settled the barrow and straightened, studying her with a mixture of confusion and anger. "Why are you angry with me?" he growled. "I thought it would please you."

"I *am* pleased," Lilith said, mopping at the tears blurring her vision. "But if you had been hurt I would not have forgiven myself."

"But I was not hurt," he said irritably. "Why are you upset about something that did not happen?"

Lilith studied him for a long moment and finally forced a chuckle, realizing that she was upset as much for herself as for him, for it had occurred to her immediately that he might have gotten himself killed trying to take down a boar bare handed and that she would be alone again. Despite what the villagers had done, she had not really been fearful since Gaelen had come back to her cottage to stay with her, because she had believed she was safe as long as he was there. The truth was she needed him far more than he needed her. "I am being silly, aren't I?" She turned to look at the barrow. "What did you get?"

She felt like weeping all over again, this time with joy, when she saw that he had brought enough flour to keep them far into the winter and salt, and fresh baked bread and seeds for planting. Laughing, she caught his face between her palms and kissed him soundly on the lips. "You are so very good at trading!" she said when she stepped back, and then danced away from him as he lifted a hand to reach for her. "Come! We must put it away quickly while there is enough light to see. We do not want the forest creatures to help themselves to it. It is a shame that you had to trade the whole boar. Roast pig would have been good after so much rabbit. But I will find the fixings for a nice stew and we will have bread!"

Chapter Ten

If Lilith had suffered any doubts before about her understanding of men, she was quickly enlightened. The impulsive kiss she had given Gaelen seemed to have fractured a barrier between them that she had carefully erected. He did not try to press her, but he took to studying her with hunger in his eyes when he thought she did not notice and she was torn between uneasiness and, as much as she hated to admit it even to herself, the desire to test him.

She had undoubtedly offended the Hawkin, for although she dashed through her bath each day and watched warily for him every time she went out, days passed with no sign of him and then a week. She told herself that she was relieved that he had decided to bother her no more with his troubles, but she knew that was not true. She was distressed. Partly it was because she had been so touched by his broken heart that she hurt for him and still yearned to soothe his hurt, but she knew that wasn't the whole of it.

She was drawn to him. She had dreams about the two of them together that woke her to a restless ache that dogged her much of every day.

It shamed her and confused her. She knew what it was. She would have been inclined to merely accept it as a rite of passage, to concede that she had come to that time when her natural life cycle was urging her to mate and produce a child, but there were several problems with that simple answer.

She had had no cycle. She knew that there was a gap in her memory from the time of the attack on her home, but she could not think that it was a very large gap, and in any case, she knew the time of her monthly cycle and that had come and gone. It might have been disrupted by the attack, but she knew it might also be because of something that had happened that she could not remember.

Beyond the fact that she was not prepared to reproduce, she was ashamed that she seemed to be as drawn to Gaelen, the man, as she was to the Hawkin. One of them, she could understand. Wanting both made her feel as if she lacked discrimination or morals, particularly since one of the things that drew her most to the Hawkin was his love for another woman.

She worked hard to put all of those anxieties from her mind, focusing on the real need to set her home to rights until it was producing the food once more that she needed to survive, for although Gaelen had said nothing about moving on, she expected him to announce most any time that he would go.

In one of her treks through the woods, she discovered the nesting place of a flock of geese. Since she no longer had livestock and was in desperate need, she studied the birds carefully for nearly a week until she found a nesting pair that was somewhat removed from the others. It was a tricky task she had set for herself, for geese were very territorial and capable of vicious attacks. That ferocity would be magnified by their determination to protect their young.

Deciding that it would be easier if she had Gaelen's help, she took him with her the day they finally finished the pen for her new chicks. For hours, they crouched in the tall grasses, watching. Finally, the male left to feed. Motioning for Gaelen to follow her, Lilith crept up as closely as she could to the nesting goose and then burst through the brush. The goose immediately let out a threatening honk, extending her long neck and arching her wings. Distracting the bird by waving one hand in front of her face, Lilith quickly grabbed the goose by the throat, dragging her from the nest.

"Take her," she said, turning to Gaelen, who merely stared at the wildly thrashing bird doubtfully. "And take care you do not hurt her. We will need her to finish hatching the goslings."

Reluctantly, he caught the goose around the throat just below Lilith's grip. When she was certain he had the bird, she knelt down quickly to gather the eggs carefully into her apron. A loud squawk distracted her. Since it was followed almost simultaneously by a roar from Gaelen, Lilith froze in her task and looked quickly around for the threat. The goose had nipped Gaelen, she saw, all up and down his hand and arm since he hadn't shifted his grip upward when she'd released the bird, and had finally managed to latch onto him hard enough he'd released his grip altogether and begun trying to shake the bird loose.

The goose, finding that she was free, attacked.

"Don't you dare hurt that bird!" Lilith yelled at Gaelen as he uttered a feral growl and swung at it with a balled fist the size of a small ham. Her apron was already half full of eggs or she would've leapt up to catch the thing again. As it was she could do nothing but watch in helpless dismay and yell directions at Gaelen, and, to make matters worse, the gander, having heard his mate's shrill honks, returned in a rush and attacked Gaelen on his flank.

Seeing that the birds were occupied, for the moment at least, with trying to chase Gaelen off, Lilith returned her attention to the nest and hurriedly gathered the last of the eggs, holding them gently, but snugly against her as she rose. The goose, discovering that Lilith had her eggs, broke off the attack on Gaelen and rushed her in a flurry of honking, thrashing wings and fiendishly determined pecks. Shielding herself with her free arm, Lilith yelped for Gaelen, who was running round in a tight circle trying to elude the gander, which had targeted his buttocks.

Hearing Lilith's cry, Gaelen changed directions abruptly and charged the goose. The goose, hearing his approach from behind, instantly whirled upon him to attack again. Lilith managed to grab the goose around the neck as she arched it back to avoid Gaelen's hand.

Panting, Lilith held the goose up for him to take her again.

Gaelen glared at her. "I will wring her neck if she bites me again," he ground out, still waving one arm to fend off the gander.

"You'll do no such thing unless you want to squat over her eggs yourself!" Lilith snapped. "We can not hatch them without her."

Uttering a growl of frustration, Gaelen took the bird, managed to subdue her and tucked her beneath one arm, trying to ignore the gander, which continued to follow him no matter how rapidly he departed, nipping at his buttocks and occasionally making a painful connection which put an added boost to Gaelen's step.

They'd nearly reached the cottage again before the gander finally gave up and both Lilith and Gaelen were huffing with the exertion of trying to outrace the gander.

Heaving a sigh of relief when she finally managed to unburden herself of the eggs inside the pen, Lilith stepped back and told Gaelen to release the goose. He looked at her suspiciously for a moment, but finally let go. The goose hit the ground, ruffled her wings furiously, and chased Gaelen around the pen several times before Lilith managed to corral her and lock her inside with her eggs.

Breathing a sigh of relief, Lilith stood watching until the goose finally climbed onto the eggs, wiggled to settle herself and uttered a few last warning honks at her attackers.

Pleased with their triumph and relieved to have the task over and done with, Lilith glanced at Gaelen. He was examining his arm and rubbing his buttocks. Abruptly, the vision of Gaelen running around in circles with the gander attached to his backside hit her and Lilith struggled with the urge to laugh. She lost.

Gaelen looked at her indignantly when she started to giggle, but that only made her laugh harder. She laughed until her sides hurt and tears began to stream down her cheeks.

After a few moments, his anger faded and a gleam of amusement lit his eyes. "I have been brutally attacked by your beasts, little bird! You find this humorous?"

Lilith bit her lip. "Poor darling! I am so sorry," she said unsteadily, mopping at her eyes, "but it not as if I did not battle them, too, and take my share of bruises ... and you looked so funny running from the gander!"

He thought back over it and chuckled. "You were funny, also. Your eyes got very big and your mouth round and then you began to flap your arm like the birds and squawk, 'Gaelen help!'"

Lilith chuckled, moving closer to him and pushing his sleeves up to examine his bruises. "Did I? Well I would not have had to if you had not let her go," she said, mock stern as she examined the red marks on his arms, rubbing them gently to take the sting away.

She didn't know why she bent her head to kiss his hurts. It was something her mother had often done to chase her tears away, but she certainly did not feel motherly toward Gaelen. She supposed that it was merely an impulse to soothe the hurt, but it was not one she should have yielded to. He stiffened when she brushed her lips lightly along his reddened skin, a fine tremor running through his arm, and she looked up at him with a mixture of self-consciousness and sudden, breathless awareness.

He swallowed thickly, his gaze moving over her face. After a moment he reached up and plucked a feather from her hair. As if he could not resist, his hand returned, smoothing her hair.

Heated desire washed through Lilith in a fiery tide. She tensed, swayed, poised for flight, fighting the urge to yield to the need she saw in his eyes and move closer. Even as she felt her inner battle sway in Gaelen's direction, however, an image of the Hawkin rose in her mind.

Swallowing against the need clogging her own throat, Lilith moved away, reluctantly at first and then rushing to escape her desire to stop and turn back. There was no real impediment to taking what she knew Gaelen was offering … except the Hawkin, whom she had no business desiring at all. It was enough that he loved another and it would be wrong to come between them, even though the woman did not seem to return his affection. But it was far worse that he was a Hawkin, a creature of the nether world. He would return to it, eventually, if he had not already.

And she did not think she could give herself to him without losing her heart.

The thought made her feel like crying. Gaelen was a worthy man, good hearted, gentle. She should not tease him with her own needs, lead him to believe she could give him something that she was afraid she couldn't.

Or worse, that she could.

She cared for him, too. He made her feel safe. He helped her without asking anything for himself beyond a pallet to sleep on and food to fill his belly. He drove away the loneliness she had not even realized she felt until he came. He did not seem to be comfortable talking about his past, but in the weeks since he had come to live with her it seemed to her that they had formed a companionable bond. Most nights, when the work was done and they had shared an evening meal, she settled in the main room of the cottage near the fire with him to attend the seemingly endless rounds of mending. And although they rarely spoke about anything beyond the chores that would need to be done the following day, or those they'd taken care of that day, his presence was enough in itself to chase away the loneliness that had dogged her days since her mother's passing.

Locking herself into her tiny bed chamber, she threw herself onto her bed and tried to sort through her chaotic emotions, listening tensely to see if Gaelen would follow her. Disappointment swept through her when he didn't, and then relief, and then frustration.

Her body tormented her almost endlessly now. She had no idea why when she had never felt the need to be with a man at all before. Now, she had begun to feel as if there was some fever inside her, eating away at her control. Every day, it seemed worse, stronger, until it seemed to have become a never ending hunger. At times, the need seemed barely noticeable, simmering beneath the surface. At others, she could scarcely train her mind away from the need that danced along her nerves until she felt like screaming.

Something had changed her. She wasn't certain if it was something natural, a life cycle that she had been unaware of before, or if something had happened to her during the time she couldn't remember.

She couldn't believe it was that, though. She didn't doubt that the villagers were perfectly capable of attacking her and using her. She'd seen the way many of the men looked at her, but they disgusted her. Nothing they could have done, she felt certain, would have changed the way she felt about them--revolted even at the idea that they had coupled with her. It certainly would not have filled her with a need there after to experience it again.

She had begun to suspect that she was breeding, though. It wasn't just that her cycle had been broken. She felt different. Her belly was swollen and tender and she felt ill and dizzy at times for no apparent reason.

She had not conceived, though, if she was indeed with child, by herself.

It was hard to decide which part of that was more difficult to accept, the possibility that she was pregnant, or the possibility that one of the villagers had gotten a child on her and so terrorized her in the process that her mind had blocked the memory.

Gaelen had disappeared by the time she nerved herself to face him again and went back to her work. Relieved to put off any sort of confrontation for a little longer, feeling horribly guilty for making him think that she would not be averse to his overtures and then dashing away, she tried to put both from her mind and focus on her chores.

He did not reappear for the evening meal, or later to find his rest on his pallet.

Nearly a week passed and Lilith had all but given up on the possibility that he would come back, when he appeared on the track one day leading a sow and her piglets.

She didn't ask him where he'd gotten them, or how. In the back of her mind, she was uneasy about any explanation he might give her. He did not seem to appreciate the general territorial attitude of most beasts, man included, and she was not all together certain that he was above simply taking it if he thought he needed it and pounding anyone who objected into the dirt.

Or if he thought it would please her to get it for her.

She recalled that she had complained that he had had to trade the boar he had killed for the bread and other supplies.

But she wondered if there had ever actually been a boar.

Gaelen was an enormous man, and seemed as strong as an ox. She thought if doing such a thing as killing a wild boar barehanded was humanly possible then Gaelen probably had the strength for it. And the story about the mire *was* plausible.

And she still wasn't convinced that it was true.

She was afraid to go to the village and find out, however.

She was only surprised angry citizens had not already descended upon her ... again.

She supposed she should have been appalled at the possibility that Gaelen was a thief. She was certainly not pleased about it, or unconcerned. But oddly enough, her fear that he might have done something wrong and that there might be a reckoning only made her feel protective of him.

She could not quite figure him out. He was intelligent. She could tell that from being around him and talking to him, but he seemed so out of his depth in everything he tried to do around the farm that he was almost child-like in other ways.

Miner or not, and she was no longer convinced that he had been, how could he have reached manhood with no notion of even how to cut wood? Or chop down a tree for that matter? He could cook, very well, and build a fire on the hearth with no trouble, and he had done wonders setting the cottage to rights, but when he had first come to stay he had had difficulty getting his clothes on correctly. As often as not, he had the shirt and breeches on backwards. She might have thought that that was intentional to save wear on the front, except that she could tell he was uncomfortable and not entirely certain why the clothing felt strange.

He seemed to figure it out fairly quickly. Where upon, he would simply strip down, turn the things around and put them on again with a complete disregard for her sensibilities, or the fact that he was standing in the yard in broad daylight at the time.

Peculiar as he was, it almost seemed his strangeness made him more endearing. She could not deny that it aroused her nurturing and protective instincts as much as his physical appeal aroused her desire.

If he had brought the sow and piglets to appease her, though, she could not tell it. He was as grouchy as a bear with an injured paw and scarcely spoke two words to her for the first few days after he had returned.

She would have apologized except that she couldn't figure out how she could manage it without admitting that she knew she had teased him and she couldn't quite bring herself to admit that. An admission, as far as she could see, would require a discussion that could easily lead to more problems in that area.

Besides, she was no longer certain of what her motives had been. She had believed at the time that she was only offering solace for his bruises and an apology for laughing at his predicament. Now she wasn't certain but that she had lied to herself, used that as an excuse to touch him and explore him, because she didn't think she would have stopped at that if she had not thought about the Hawkin at just that moment.

She had finally been forced to admit to herself, though, that she wanted the Hawkin more even than Gaelen. She had no idea why. In his own way, he was as handsome a creature as Gaelen, perhaps even more, because there was also the appeal of the mysterious and exotic, but she did not think it was merely physical appeal.

She could not help but wonder, though, if it was nothing more than the sheer contrariness of human nature to want what one could not or should not have. She did not like to think that that was the case. She did not believe it was. It seemed to her that it was more an empathy for his hurt, a need to soothe, admiration for his nobility in freeing his love even when it caused him pain to do so, and the yearning to have for herself what he had offered another-- love without boundaries. It did not seem to her that there were many who had so much to give, in her own world or his.

Her mother had certainly not found it, for she had discovered that the man she loved belonged to another in truth, that the man who had gotten her with child was already wed and had a family.

She knew that that was not something she need be concerned about with the Hawkin. She thought that that was probably true of Gaelen, as well, though, and he would not be torn between living in her world and his.

It would be best, she finally decided, not to meddle in the Hawkin's affairs, assuming, of course, that he had not already returned to the nether world. It was not her place to ease his wounds. In time, he would either convince his lady to love him, or he would recover without her interference and she would not risk being caught in the middle.

Unfortunately, she realized only a few weeks later that she had no business encouraging Gaelen either. When she passed her second woman's time with no cycle, she knew she had to be breeding and she did not think, even as kind and good natured as Gaelen was that he would accept her when he discovered she was carrying another man's child. It was unfair, of course. She knew, even though she could not remember how or when it had happened, that she had not sought this, and it hardly seemed just that she and the baby would both be considered wicked for something they could not help, but life was not fair.

No doubt, the villagers would either claim that she had lain with demons, or that she had placed a spell on some man and stolen his seed for evil purposes.

They already despised her, though, and she thought it doubtful they could have any lower opinion of her, but the baby--she hated to think that it would have to suffer their cruelties.

She was glad, at least, that she had no memory of the coupling. If it *had* been one of the villagers as she thought, then she was certain she preferred not to know the identity of the father. And she was just as certain that it would make it far easier to accept and love her child thinking of it only as her own.

She was miserable to think that she could not be with either man now, though. If she had not met them, she would probably be overjoyed to discover that she was with child, that she would finally have someone to love who would love her. She was still happy. She knew she was, but she enjoyed Gaelen's company and it would be hard to lose him now when she had grown accustomed to having him with her.

He had withdrawn from her already, though, after the incident with the geese, and she decided she must have chased away the Hawkin, as well, for she had not seen him in weeks.

She supposed, she thought one day as she worked in her garden, that she was already growing accustomed to being alone again. Gaelen spent more time watching her in brooding silence than speaking to her. If not for the fact that she had realized she was breeding, she would have tried to mend their fences, but that had changed everything.

Pausing when she reached the end of a row, she straightened, placing a hand to her back to ease the pain and arching against it.

A flash of white caught her gaze as she bent to her task again, and she stopped, lifting her head to look.

One of the village men was standing at the edge of her yard, watching her intently. She did not know his name, but she recognized him, for she rarely managed to make a trip to the village and back again without running afoul of him. Twice, he had accosted her. The first time, his wife had opportunely called to him and diverted him long enough for her to make her escape. The second time, he had lain in wait for her beyond the edge of the village. She had only escaped him then because Pig had routed him.

She glared at him, her belly tightening with nausea as it occurred to her for the first time to wonder if he had fathered her child. Errant bits and pieces of memory descended upon her abruptly as she stared at him, of the villagers, angry and threatening, closing in around her.

He'd been at the forefront, calling her a witch, accusing her of bespelling them all.

The memories rocked her, but she could not seem to turn her mind away from them. She continued to struggle to piece the tidbits together, to try to understand what had happened afterward, after they had threatened, after they had stolen her flock and her pig. There was darkness there, though, that she could not breach.

"You look none the worse for wear," he murmured.

Lilith blinked, coming out of her reverie abruptly and discovering that he had closed the distance between them while she was frozen with fear and caught up in the maelstrom of memories whirling through her mind.

"What do you mean by that?" she asked tightly, knowing that it was an insult, however thinly veiled, suspecting that he referred to the incident she had only just remembered.

"Did yon monolith help you to escape?" he asked, jerking his chin in the direction of the village. "Is that how you managed to get out of the cave of the beasts?"

Lilith stared at him in horror as two facts emerged from his questions--Gaelen must be in the village, or he would not have dared to come--and he believed she had been in the Labyrinth.

Had she? Why would he think she had been there if he had not had something to do with taking her there? No one went willingly, and she had heard that many of the villages had taken their unwanted there for the beasts, the demons. None had ever returned, though.

Except her mother.

"Or maybe you really are a witch?"

"You have doubts now?" Lilith retorted, standing her ground with an effort, casting about in her mind a little frantically to think what to do to protect herself from him. He was too close, though. She had been distracted and he had gotten too close either for her to try to swing the hoe at him or to run. He would catch her before she managed to do either one.

He chuckled, showing broken, blackened teeth that made her feel even more ill. "I never thought you were."

Anger surged through her. "But you accused me in front

of everyone in the village! You incited them to attack me!"

He grew angry, as well. "Everyone accused you. If I had not, then they would have believed that I was bespelled by you, or worse, in league!"

"Coward!" Lilith spat at him. "Spineless cur! Get out of my yard! Leave!" she screamed at him.

"Not until I get what I came for," he snarled, surging toward her before the words were even out of his mouth and grabbing her. "You have flaunted yourself in front of me for years. If you have taken a man to your bed already, you can have no objections to taking another."

Rage went through Lilith. She swung at him with the hoe, but it was too late to have any effect at all upon him, for he'd grabbed her arms and she could not draw her arm back far enough to put any force into the blows. She flailed at him anyway as they struggled back and forth, stomping down the garden she had worked so hard on. Finally, he released her long enough to snatch her bludgeon out of her grip, tearing the flesh of her palms in the process.

She hardly noticed the pain. The moment he let go of her, she whirled and ran. He caught up to her within a couple of strides, slamming into her from behind and sending them both to the ground. She threw dirt in his face as he leaned away from her to roll her over. He spluttered and blinked, trying to dislodge the dirt from his eyes and finally let go of her arms to rub his eyes. She struggled backwards, using her elbows to try to tug free of his weight. Before she'd managed to make much progress, however, he'd wiped the dirt from his eyes and launched himself down on her, using his superior weight to pin her to the ground.

She slapped at him, pulling at his long, stringy hair and clawing at his face as she felt his hands reaching into her bodice. She screamed again, more from fury than fear, trying to bite him when her slapping and pulling at his hair seemed to have little effect. Balling one hand into a fist, he swung at her, but missed as he was abruptly yanked back and upwards.

Panting, in too much shock to fully comprehend what had happened, Lilith scrambled to her feet and ran to get the hoe he'd flung away. She turned just in time to see the villager whirl toward Gaelen, who'd pulled him off of her, and drive a knife into Gaelen's belly.

A stunned look came over Gaelen's face. Bright red blood gushed from his side. Lilith screamed in real terror then. Certain the man had killed Gaelen, she rushed back to the struggling men and whacked the villager on the back of his head with the hoe handle. Gaelen, either from surprise or weakness, released the man at almost the same moment. Her attacker staggered back, turning in a drunken circle to stare at her in stupefied surprise as he lifted a hand to the knot she'd put on his skull with the handle of the hoe.

Chapter Eleven

"Go!" Lilith screamed, swinging at the man again and following him as he jumped back to avoid the hoe. The man stared at her. Abruptly, his eyes widened until they looked like they would bulge from his head.

Lilith swung at him again, connecting so hard with his shoulder as he whirled to run that it sent jarring pain shooting from her hands to her elbows. "Coward!" she screamed after him as he began to run down the track as fast as he could manage at his wobbling gait. When she was certain he would not stop and turn back, she dropped the hoe and turned, rushing to Gaelen.

She could tell nothing about his expression, but she burst into tears when she saw the blood on his shirt. "You're hurt! Oh, Gaelen! It looks--let me see," she babbled, tugging at his shirt and pulling it away from his skin. The wound had closed, but she felt little comfort in it, for knife wounds often did. She could not recall to save her life--or Gaelen's--how big the knife had been, or calculate how deeply he might have been wounded. Deep enough to puncture something vital so that he bled to death? Or deep enough to give him a slow, agonizing death?

He looked bemused when she wrapped at arm around his waist to help him into the cottage. "Let me help you inside so that I can have a better look," she said shakily.

"It is not bad."

She uttered a sob, but fought the urge to fall apart. She would be useless to him if she did. It was something of a relief that he seemed to manage well enough with her help, but she worried that he was using strength he could not afford to lose for fear of putting too much of his weight on her.

She had to mop the tears from her face even to see him once she had gotten him to sit down on his pallet and then helped him to stretch out. Lifting his shirt again, she carefully probed the wound. To her surprise and relief she discovered that it was not deep at all, hardly more than a skin break. Biting her lip, she studied the wound for several moments and finally got up to get water, fearing that the blood had merely caused the flesh to stick together.

She had no idea what she would do if she found that was the case, because if he was damaged inside no potion that she knew of would close and heal such a wound, but she had to know if he was dying. Grabbing water from the pot beside the hearth and a clean cloth, she rinsed the drying blood from him and probed the wound again. It had either closed, and very tightly, or he had only been scraped by the knife for she could not open it. She sat back on her heels, wondering if it was safe to feel the relief that had begun to take hold of her.

"I told you that it was not bad."

She looked at his face then. Bursting into tears, she flung herself down on his broad chest. "I thought he had killed you," she said between wracking sobs. "I don't know what I would have done if he had … if he had…."

He lay motionless for several moments and finally tugged her upward so that her face was against his neck and she was lying against him more comfortably. He began to stroke her back soothingly. "Hush, little bird. It makes me … ache to hear you cry. I was not hurt."

She sniffed, trying to regain control. "That snake! To pull a knife on an unarmed man! I should have pulverized him with the hoe!"

"You are hurt?" he said after a moment, anger beginning to thread his voice.

Lilith sniffed. "Bruises, I suppose. I was so angry I hardly noticed, and then worried about you."

He shifted after a moment, pushing her until she was lying beside him, and then examined her face and head, running his hands down her arms to check them. He paused, frowning, when he looked at her palms. After stroking the angry red marks lightly with his fingers for a moment, he lifted the hand he held and kissed her palm lightly.

Lilith felt her belly tighten at his touch. She curled her fingers to touch his cheek.

When he lifted his head, he turned to meet her gaze and Lilith caught her breath. The urge to rise up to meet him was so strong Lilith found it nigh irresistible. She might have acted on it except for the fact that her conscience chose that inopportune moment to give voice to the doubts that had been troubling her for days.

She looked away. She didn't want to tell him she was carrying some other man's child, not now of all times.

But wouldn't it be worse not to say anything now and leave him to discover it on his own? He might not forgive her if she lied to him by omission.

He might not anyway.

The only thing that could possibly be worse would be to not tell him at all and allow him to believe the child was his. And he was bound to if she was so lost to decency as to give herself to him now without telling him, for she could not be far along at all.

The wicked desire to deceive Gaelen swept through her so strongly that she sat up abruptly and moved away from him, struggling with her conscience, with the urge to confess, and the fear that to do so would ruin any chance that they might be together.

"What troubles you?"

Lilith glanced at him sharply, biting her lip. She was *such* a coward! She could not gather the nerve to tell him for fear he would look at her with loathing and disgust and she could not go to him for the same reason. And he could not understand if she told him nothing at all. He would only be hurt, thinking that she had rejected him again.

Of all the unpalatable choices open to her, which would be worse?

"I will find the man and kill him if you are afraid that he will return," he said after a long moment.

Lilith gaped at him. "No!"

He frowned. "You care for the man?"

"Certainly not! I felt like killing him myself, but you do not take a life unless a life has been taken! He attacked and he was soundly beaten. It is punishment enough--that and his life, for I have seen his wife and she is an ill tempered female. Not but what she probably has reason to be for he is shiftless and lazy besides being a coward."

He shrugged. "If it is as you say, then he will be no great loss."

"*You* would be a great loss, though!" Lilith exclaimed worriedly. "I would lose you and … and I do not think I could bear that. They would not let his death go unpunished. Leave it. He is not worth it and I am not worried he will come back any time soon."

Galen considered that in frowning silence for a moment. He was fairly certain the knave would not be back either, for he had made certain the man knew exactly whom he would be dealing with, half shifting into his true form so that the man could be in no doubt that he was the Hawkin who had already proclaimed Lilith as his own. "You care for me?"

Lilith bit her lip. "Of course I do! How could you think otherwise when I have been weeping all over you from fear that you were badly hurt?"

"I am confused," Gaelen said irritably, wondering why, if she spoke the truth, she was standing on the other side of the room from him instead of making love with him.

Lilith looked at him helplessly for a moment and finally spoke in a rush. "I am with child!" she said baldly.

He looked perfectly blank, as well he might, for he had no reason to believe that she had ever had any man around.

"I don't know how it happened," she added hurriedly, hopeful that if she could explain quickly enough that she could get it said before he exploded in anger. "At least, I am sure I do, except that I do not remember. I woke in the woods naked, and I did not remember anything."

Gaelen stared at Lilith with a frozen look of dismay as he realized abruptly that he had fallen into a trap of his own making. In truth, he had not thought beyond discovering if he would be more pleasing to her if he looked like a man, but she had accepted him, welcomed his help and his companionship and he had been lulled by a false sense of security into believing that, at last, he had found the way to win her love.

He could not think what to do or say, but he could see that she was waiting for him to say something.

'I know' seemed like the worst possibility, for then she would wonder why, and she had been enraged with him, he remembered belatedly, when she had discovered before that he had deceived her about his knowledge of her mother. He did not think that she would be relieved and happy now if he said that he knew she was breeding because the child was his. It seemed far more likely that she would become enraged with him and demand that he go.

Frustration surged through him. He enjoyed pain as much as the next demon, but he had not endured this kind of torture before and he was beginning to think he would go mad if she continued to tease him and then change her mind just when she seemed about to give herself to him.

He did not understand mortals at all, and he especially did not understand mortal women.

He was tempted to simply tell her that he had deceived her and have an end to it.

Somehow, though, he could not seem to bring himself to do that.

She had said she cared for him. Perhaps, if he contained his impatience only a little longer something would come to him and he would think of a way either to explain to her why he had done it so that she would not be enraged with him.

Or he would become more adept and she would never find out.

He rather thought it might be best if she never found out, for he had a feeling that time would do nothing to mitigate her anger if she did.

"You are angry with me," she said tentatively.

Brought abruptly from his unpleasant thoughts, Gaelen did his best to clear his expression. "Nay," he denied at once, knowing there was a trap lying in wait for him somewhere in that comment, but not entirely certain of what it was or how he was going to avoid falling into it.

"I saw it in your eyes," she said accusingly.

"I was thinking."

Her eyes narrowed. "You were thinking that I am a loose woman."

He was not thinking any such thing, he thought indignantly, because he had no idea what in Hades she was talking about. He thought it would not be prudent to point out to her that *he* could read minds, though, and that it was not an ability that she could claim.

"Nay, I was not!" he protested a little weakly, trying to figure out what a loose woman was and wondering what that had to do with him being angry and her being with child.

He was in no mood to try to think what it might mean. In the first place, his desire for her was frying his brain and he could not think much beyond that, and in the second place he was certain he did not care.

He also did not care for the way she was looking at him at the moment, however, and he struggled valiantly to prod his sluggish brain into functioning.

After a brief struggle, he vaguely recalled a discussion between them some time before when she had said something about mating and only one woman, or something to that effect. But he could not really recall it with any clarity. Because from the moment she had mentioned mating he had not been able to think of anything beyond the painful throbbing in his groin and the way her breasts rose above the thing she wore each time she took a deep breath.

It would be easier to say what she wanted him to say, he decided angrily, if she would only give him more of a clue of what she was upset about.

She sniffed. "I knew that you would look at me like that if I told you!" she said angrily and stalked from the room, slamming the door to her bed chamber.

He scowled at the door for several moments, sorely tempted to rip it from its hinges and toss it into the yard. Finally, regaining control of his temper somewhat, he got to his feet and stalked from the cottage to strip the annoying man things from his body and sit in the icy stream to cool his ballocks and curse mankind for the contrary, obstinate beasts that they were.

* * * *

Lilith plopped on the edge of her bed and stared at the mote of light that pierced the shutters over her window and formed a tiny circle on the rag rug that she and her mother had made together. She felt strangely detached from herself, rather like someone who had been struck so hard out of the blue that their mind had not yet been able to register the pain.

She had tried to convince herself that Gaelen would not judge her, that he would accept her even if he knew that she was carrying a child that belonged to another man. He had never been anything but kind and understanding and she could not believe that he was being so unforgiving and judgmental now.

She tried to decide whether she felt more hurt or angry, but finally realized that all she really felt was lost and empty. Regret swept through her. She knew that she had done the right thing in telling him, and she did not think she could have done anything else and lived with herself, but she wished now that she had waited.

There had been so many clashes between them of late that the harmony they had shared at first had already been strained. If she had waited a while before she told him then, perhaps, he would have had an easier time accepting.

Perhaps not, but she would still have had more time with him.

It dawned on her with that thought exactly how she felt. Bereft, because she was afraid that he would leave now and she had no idea how she might convince him to stay.

She felt like crying when she heard him get up and stalk from the cottage. It took all she could do to keep from leaping to her feet and chasing after him to beg him to stay.

Some of the tension left her when she had sat for a while, listening to see if he would come back, not because she was relieved when he didn't, but simply because she was too worn out to maintain it any longer.

Restlessness followed on the heels of her relief from the extreme distress and finally she got up and left the cottage, unable to bear being cooped up inside any longer. Taking one of the paths that led from the clearing around the cottage, she followed it without purpose, thinking of nothing in particular.

She realized, though, when she came upon the place where she had awakened to find the Hawkin staring at her and no memory of her trek to the spot that her stroll had not been without purpose. She stared at the place for some time, looking around as she struggled to open her mind to memories that would not come.

Giving up after a time, she left the place and followed the meandering path until she found herself standing at the edge of the meadow where she often gathered her herbs. Late flowers swayed in the faint breeze that brushed over their crowns.

She had met the Hawkin again just here, she realized. She had been searching for herbs and edible roots and she had felt his gaze upon her and looked up. He had seemed so forlorn she had felt her fear dissipate, had felt compelled to go to him.

When it dawned on her that she had come in hopes that she would see him, she frowned and moved deeper into the meadow and finally sat among the wildflowers. She had no idea how long she sat, thinking of nothing in particular when a shadow overhead caught her attention. When she looked up, she saw the Hawkin. Her heart skipped several beats in gladness, and awe.

He was a beautiful creature as he soared and dipped in the sky far above her, graceful as she had never seen him before. She had not given much thought, she realized, to the fact that he was not earth bound as she was, that the sky was more his element than the earth. In truth, he was far more graceful even when he walked as men walked than most of the men she had had the opportunity to observe.

As she leaned back to watch him, bracing herself on her arms, he circled lower and lower and finally landed only a little way from where she sat. Tramping through the high grasses he approached her purposefully and finally knelt down on his knees little more than two arms lengths from where she sat, studying her for a long time.

She hadn't realized how much she had missed him.

"You do not make the sound in your throat that you usually do when you are here," he said finally, his voice almost tentative.

Lilith felt a flicker of surprise. She sat up, prodding her mind for what he meant. "Humming?"

He seemed almost to shrug. "Singing without speaking words."

"Today I am not happy."

He frowned, but thoughtfully. "Why?"

She shook her head. She had no desire to talk about it. "I have not seen you in a very long time. Did I … was it something that I said that made you go away? Or is it because you have been with your lady love?"

He seemed disconcerted by the questions. "I have not been with her," he responded finally, scrubbing his palms almost restlessly along his hard thighs. "She will have none of me and I … ache with my need until I can scarcely think, until my body burns and my mind is afire."

She should have been horrified, she supposed, perhaps even disgusted by his frank discussion of his needs. Instead, every word seemed to summon heat from her own body. She had need, too, desperate need. Mayhap that was at least a part of why her mind was so disordered?

She did not know and she found she did not care either. She had long passed the need to rationalize the cravings inside of her, or excuse them. He was right. It *was* a need, just as the air was a need, and water, and food, and she was weary with aching with the relentless, nearly unbearable hunger.

Rising, she moved to him almost like a sleepwalker and knelt to face him.

Why should he suffer only because the woman he wanted was a fool who did not appreciate him?

Why should she deny what she wanted only because of some notion that it was morally wrong? Why and how could it be wrong to behave as nature intended?

Holding his gaze, she lifted her hands and touched his arms lightly with her fingers. His skin felt as silken as it looked, she discovered. The long, bulging muscles felt as hard as she had thought they would, and yet yielding, warm to the touch.

A tremor went through him. His eyes glazed as she explored him, first his arms, and then the muscles of his chest. After a moment, she sat back on her heels, studying him for any sign that he meant to reject her offer. When she saw only a tense waiting, as if he was holding his breath, she loosened the lacings on the back of her gown and peeled it off. Tossing it aside, she removed her chemise and corset.

He caught her arms as she untied the draw string of her pantalets, bearing her backwards until she was lying in the grasses, pressing his body against hers until her breasts were flattened between them, throbbing with the blood pounding through her. His mouth claimed hers almost with savagery, with an impatience to explore the tender cavern of her mouth with his tongue that sucked the breath from her lungs. Dizziness swept through her as she tasted his essence on her tongue, inhaled his scent into her lungs so that it seemed to mingle with her blood, set fire to it.

She kissed him back, entwining her tongue with his as she skimmed her palms up the unyielding muscles of his upper arms that knotted with the weight he supported with them, over the rounded knob of his shoulders, and across the ropy connective tissue to his neck. Looping her arms around his neck briefly, she tightened them, moving closer to him, sucking on his tongue hungrily as the fire inside her grew quickly to a blaze.

The tremors rippling through him grew more pronounced. He broke the contact with her mouth and leaned away to cover one breast instead, tugging on it with his lips and mouth and tongue and sending an explosion of keen sensation through her. The fire gathered in her belly. The muscles of her sex flexed and contracted rhythmically with the need for his flesh. Heated moisture gathered there to ease his possession, weeping for it.

Uttering a sound of impatience and eagerness, she shifted to assist his efforts as he tugged her pantalets off and thrust a knee between her bare thighs. She arched, rubbing her sex along his thigh to ease the ache of her nether lips, swollen now and acutely, almost painfully, sensitive.

He shuddered. Releasing the nipple he had teased until she thought she would go mad, he paused, lifting his head to drag in several harsh breaths as if he was struggling for control. He sought her other breast after a moment, teasing it as he had the first until she began to move ceaselessly beneath his touch, moaning with the ache that his every caress built inside her mercilessly. The feel of his mouth and tongue pushed her relentlessly beyond awareness of anything beyond his lovemaking. The knot of tension inside of her that coiled tightly at his first touch grew quickly tighter and tighter until she felt as if she would be crushed beneath the pressure it built in her. And yet it seemed to expand for all that, until it encompassed her and she felt herself hovering maddeningly near the brink of release, unable to cross, unable to cool or find even the slightest ease from the tension as his palms moved over her, his lips, as she felt the faintly rough tease of his tongue against her skin.

She was aware of everything about him and yet the pleasure seemed to pound through her from every direction, and her mind swirled with the intoxication of her senses, dulling her to the purposefulness of his exploration until she felt his mouth along her upper thigh. She sucked in a sharp breath at the jolt that quaked through her. "Gaelen! Don't!"

He hesitated, lifted his head to look up at her.

She swallowed against the hard knot of need in her throat, wanting to feel him there and yet reluctant to yield the lure of having him inside of her. "I want your flesh inside of me," she said shakily.

"A taste, little bird," he said, dragging his gaze from hers and staring hungrily at the delicate pink flesh he had exposed when he had pushed her thighs wide. "Only a taste."

She shuddered, feeling her belly clench eagerly at his

request. "I can not hold back," she said a little desperately.

"Then do not," he murmured, lowering his mouth to her and sucking at the ring in her flesh, pulling the ring and her bud into his mouth. She grunted almost in pain as the scorching heat of his mouth sent a hard shock jolting through her, arching her head back and tensing all over, fighting the warning tremors that quaked through her as he sucked and tugged at her, ravenous with his own need.

In moments, as she had feared, hoped, euphoria burst inside of her explosively. Her belly clenched so hard with the release that it skated the edge of pain. She gasped, sobbed as her body was wracked by hard waves of rapture.

It seemed to go on endlessly as he continued to lathe her with his tongue and suck on the bud--and yet ended far too soon. A vague dissatisfaction swept through her even as she went limp in the aftermath.

Settling her feet to the ground when she ceased to thrash and groan with release, he moved up her body as he had moved down, exploring her with his hands, his lips, his tongue, nipping and teasing her flesh with the edge of his teeth. She shuddered, jerked, feeling far more sensitive even than she had felt before, uncertain of whether the reawakening of her senses was welcome or not.

By the time he reached her breasts and began to tease them again, she was no longer in any doubt. From the ashes of spent passion, embers glowed, caught fire, blazing hotter than before. She stroked and explored his body feverishly, encouraging him, demanding to feel him inside her.

She felt almost ill with need by the time she felt his cock head pushing into her. Eagerly, she lifted her hips to meet his thrust, groaning as she felt her body begin to engulf his flesh. Hungry for more, she bucked as he withdrew and then advanced again, sinking deeper.

He wasn't giving her enough, fast enough. She caught his buttocks, struggling against her own resisting flesh to sheathe him fully. He shuddered, stilled for a moment, gasping hoarsely.

Abruptly, he yielded to her insistent demand, driving deeply. She gasped sharply as his engorged flesh impaled her, her nails digging into him. Groaning hoarsely, he withdrew slightly and drove into her again, his control slipping further and further from his grip until he set a frantic, pounding pace.

She hung onto him tightly, her rising passion keeping pace with his, outstripping his. Her body had already begun to convulse with release when she felt his begin to quake and spasm.

Weak when the waves stopped rocking her, she loosened her frantic hold on him and allowed her arms to drop limply to the ground at her sides. He settled closer, his arms still bearing the bulk of his weight, but his chest resting heavily against hers, pressing into her with each harsh breath he dragged into his lungs.

When his breath had steadied somewhat, he nuzzled his face against the side of her neck, nipping at her skin with his lips. Her flesh prickled, tightened. She groaned, instantly at war with herself, wanting more, certain she was too exhausted to feel more.

She found that she wasn't. He stirred the heat inside of her again, took her to the heights of passion until waves of euphoria broke over her, and then took her there again as if he could not get enough of her and each coupling only fed his need for more.

Chapter Twelve

The gloom of evening was already crawling across the forest when Lilith became aware of her surroundings. Lazily, she opened her eyes and stared up at the trees above her for several moments before it dawned on her that she didn't remember being in the forest, let alone falling asleep there.

Pushing herself up on her elbows, she saw that her clothing was balled beside her.

Dimly at first, and then more strongly, she recalled the sensation of being carried.

Smiling faintly, relaxing, she lay back, stretching, frowning at the tender pull of muscles along her thighs. She felt--wonderful, she realized, exhausted, sore, but oddly peaceful. Her body tingled and pricked at the memory of the Hawkin's touch--Gaelen's.

She frowned at that. What were the odds, she wondered, that two men would come into her life named Gaelen? Or rather, a man and a Hawkin?

She had puzzled over it before, but aside from the oddity of it, hadn't really considered it. If coincidence was not commonplace there would have been no word for it, after all.

Dismissing her thoughts after a moment, she sorted her clothes and pulled them on. She thought she would have been happy to lie where she was, reliving the moments in the meadow, but it was growing dark and she found that she was starving.

Her thighs quivered as she trudged back to her cottage, reminding her with every step of Gaelen's hips between them, of his engorged flesh plowing into her.

She was worn down with weariness, and yet the more she thought about it, the harder the craving became to go to him again.

A little uneasy with her thoughts, she set them aside again as she crossed the yard and pushed the door to the cottage open. Gaelen, the man, was crouched at the hearth, stirring food in her cook pot. He glanced at her as she came in, but returned his attention to the food almost at once.

Guilt swept over her. She had angered him and hurt him and then she had fled into the arms of another man--being.

She should have stopped by the brook to bathe, she realized belatedly. She could still smell him on her flesh, but she hadn't *wanted* to bathe his scent from her. She had wanted to wrap herself in it to hug the memories to herself.

Moving to one of the chairs at the table after a moment, she plopped down in it weakly. "I am sorry," she said tentatively after watching his stiff back for several moments.

He didn't look at her, but she could see that he was frowning. "Why?" he asked gruffly.

"I was unreasonable," she confessed. When he said nothing, she continued. "I have not … seemed myself lately. I do not *know* myself any more. It is almost as if I am someone else, changed from the person I once was."

He said nothing for several moments, as if he was feeling his way carefully around a hazard. "You are breeding," he responded, his voice rough.

Lilith swallowed against the knot that formed in her throat. "Do you think it is that?"

He glanced at her and then looked away again. Finally, he merely shrugged.

The knot grew until it was hard to swallow. "Do you hate me for it?"

He whirled at that, his expression eloquent of dumbfounded surprise. "Why would I hate you?"

She studied his face for several moments and then looked

down at her hands, feeling a mixture of relief and more guilt. She had betrayed her feelings for him. She had struck him out of the blue with her announcement and then been angry with him because he was stunned and could not think of the way to respond that would please her and ease her mind.

And then, she had rushed off to the Hawkin.

She could *not* confess that! He would think she had only done it to punish him.

And the worst of it was, she had not. She had not even thought of him when the Hawkin had appeared to her. She had thought of nothing beyond giving him the comfort he needed and taking for herself.

"Your skin is red," he said abruptly.

She looked down self-consciously, realizing that she had cavorted in the meadow until the sun had burned her skin. She blushed, cleared her throat. "I was …uh … in the meadow. The sun burned me."

He took the food from the hearth and brought it to the table. Lilith leapt up at once and began to gather plates and mugs of water and utensils to eat with. "Eat, little bird," he said gently when she merely stared at the food on her plate.

She glanced at him sharply at that, recalling abruptly that the Hawkin had called her little bird. She thought he had anyway. Had he? Or was her mind playing tricks upon her again? Frowning thoughtfully, she picked up her knife and cut a slice from the meat he had placed before her, finding as she ate that her appetite had returned with a vengeance.

When they had finished, she gathered the dirty plates and mugs and headed down to the brook to clean them. Setting them aside when she had finished, she glanced uncertainly toward the cottage and finally removed her clothes and stepped into the edge of the stream to bathe.

"You will need these," Gaelen said abruptly.

Jerking all over since she had been too preoccupied to notice his approach, Lilith turned and watched him tensely as he covered the distance that separated them and squatted down, handing her a wash cloth and soap. Disconcerted, she took them wordlessly.

He settled on a fallen log close by as if he had only come to watch and could think of no reason why she should object.

After a moment, realizing that she was not particularly unsettled by his familiarity, Lilith lathered the cloth.

"Why were you angry before? You do not want the child?"

Lilith glanced at him in surprise but returned her attention to lathering herself after that quick look. She wished the water was not so cold it made her skin pucker and her teeth rattle.

"Truthfully, I do not know. I might be more certain if I knew the father," she mumbled.

"It is *your* child. You would not want it if you ... did not care for the father?"

She looked down at her stomach. The rounding was so faint that she doubted that she would even have noticed if she had not known her own body so well. "I do not think I have accustomed myself to the thought that it is really there," she said finally. "I mean--I know it is, but it does not seem real. I do not know. Mayhap, in time, I will want it regardless, only for itself. Now, I can not think about the child without also thinking about the father. I would be ... ill if I discovered it was that lout who attacked us."

"Happily, it is not," he ground out, anger threading his voice suddenly.

Lilith sent him a surprised look. "How would you know that?"

He studied her for a long moment, but said no more.

"You saw!" she exclaimed. "You were in the forest when it ... happened!"

He got up. "Nothing happened to you in the forest," he said tightly, rising abruptly and stalking off in the direction of the cottage.

She frowned angrily when he left, but got out of the water, dried herself and then slipped into her pantalets and chemise. After a moment's consideration, she decided not to put on the corset and dress.

Wryly, she thought that if she was naked and had not incited Gaelen to violent ardor she was not likely to in her chemise and she wanted fresh clothing after her bath. She would not have put anything at all on except for the fear that the lout from the village might have come back to stare at her.

Gaelen was sitting before the hearth when she returned, staring into the flames as if he was mesmerized by the dancing light. She ignored him, crossing the cottage to her bed chamber where she tossed off the clothes she had just put on and changed into a night dress.

She was tired, but restless. When she had blown out the lamp and settled she found herself staring at the low ceiling above her instead of closing her eyes. She was miffed, she realized, that Gaelen had seemed so indifferent to her. She thought she had detected a gleam of appreciation in his eyes a couple of times when she had glanced at him, but she did not know if it was true, or if she was only trying to comfort herself with a lie.

He had not seemed indifferent to her before.

But mayhap that was only her imagination, too? She had been walking about like a she-beast in heat for weeks, fighting the craving she felt to have a man between her thighs. Mayhap she had only thought he looked at her with the same hunger?

He had not told her how he felt about the child, she realized suddenly.

He had only asked how she felt about the child.

Mayhap that meant that he was not certain how he felt about her condition either?

He had not been angry, she remembered, at least not until

she had mentioned her fear that the lout from the village might have gotten his child on her. He had not liked that. She supposed that accounted for his flat denial that the man could be responsible, not, as she had at first thought because he had been there and seen, but because it revolted every feeling to consider it a possibility.

She would almost have felt better, though, if she *had* believed he had said it because he knew, because he had seen who had assaulted her.

But he had said nothing had happened in the forest, she remembered.

He had not been there as far as she knew. She had met him later, when the villagers had come back and she'd fled into the woods to hide.

She puzzled over it for some moments and finally dismissed it. Most likely it was like his denial about the father of the child. He simply preferred not to think it had happened or he was trying to convince her because he knew how upsetting it was for her.

She preferred it too. The problem was, something had most definitely happened, and she knew it must have been bad if she could not remember.

Despite her anxieties, Lilith slept far better once she fell asleep than she had in many days and woke feeling more refreshed and ready to face the day. For all that, she found her mind wandering to the Hawkin as she went about her chores.

She could not help but feel a little guilty about what she had done, partly because of Gaelen and partly because of the woman that the Hawkin truly loved, but she decided that she need not heed her conscience. What she had done was not wrong. She had made no commitment to Gaelen, nor any promises.

She certainly had no reason to feel guilty about the love of the Hawkin's life, for the woman had rejected him after all. If she did not care for him, then she had no claim to be jumped.

She supposed after a while that it was not really guilt plaguing her. She felt badly because she did feel a great deal of affection toward Gaelen and she was worried because she knew she had done far more than merely expend her passion with the Hawkin. She had taken a step that she was probably going to regret.

Because, despite the fact that she knew her urges were natural, she did not think she would be able to get away with merely easing her needs with the Hawkin and then simply dismissing him from her life when he went away. She was going to be hurt. He had already touched something deep inside of her when she had learned of his plight. She cared for him, as much as she did Gaelen, perhaps even more.

She was an unreasonable creature, though. No matter how many times she told herself to put it from her mind and stay away from the Hawkin, for everyone's sake, the urge grew stronger every day to go into the forest again in hopes of meeting him.

She managed to fight the urge for almost a week, and then woke one morning with an absolute and irresistible determination to see him again. Her premeditation about it unsettled her, but she primped for her lover anyway, grabbed a basket and headed for the meadow, breathless with anticipation before she had even quit the yard.

She made a pretense of gathering herbs and roots but the moment she saw the Hawkin, she dropped the basket and went to him shamelessly, greeting him by brazenly slipping one hand upward to cup his neck and urge him to lean down to kiss her and the other downward to wrap her fingers around his already turgid man root.

She was heavy with need, quaking with it, breathless, her heart thundering in her ears before she even touched him. The moment she felt his lips on hers, tasted him, fisted her hand around his hot member, she was lost to all else, filled with a dark, mindless hunger that demanded to be assuaged. Pressing closely to him, she explored his mouth as thoroughly as he explored hers, stroking his cock and then moving her hand downwards to cup his ballocks gently and massage them. He jerked as she began to rub him there. A quiver went through his body that sent an answering rush of heat through her. When she broke the kiss at last, it was to explore his body as he had hers before, with her palms and fingers, with her lips and tongue.

The taste and texture of his flesh sent her spiraling further out of control, heightened her need. Kneeling at last, she took his distended flesh into her mouth, sucking him greedily, stroking him with her hands. The tremors running through him grew, became hard quakes. He swayed, placing his hands on her shoulders to steady himself.

Exhilarated by his response, feeling her own body coiling more tightly toward culmination, she intensified her efforts, taking him as deeply into her mouth as she could, stroking him faster. His hands tightened on her shoulders, bit into them bruisingly as his body crested. He uttered a groan that was half sob as his cock jerked in her mouth and began to pump his seed from his body. She stroked and sucked at him feverishly until she had milked him dry.

His knees buckled as she lifted her head.

She gave him a moment to catch his breath and leaned down, taking his flaccid member into her mouth and teasing him until it grew turgid once more. His hand tangled in her hair, pulling her up. She yielded to the tug, the demand. Rising up to loop an arm around his neck, she lifted her skirts and pressed his manhood between her thighs, tracing the slit in the crotch of her pantalets until she had aligned their bodies.

His own breath nearly as ragged as hers already, he slipped his hands beneath her skirts, caught her hips in his broad hands and lifted her up until she could wrap her legs around his waist. She tightened her arms around his neck, allowing gravity and his thrusts to claim her. A groan scraped from her throat as he claimed her completely.

"Gaelen," she murmured against his neck. "It feels so good to have you inside of me."

He ground his teeth, swayed and finally wrapped an arm around her waist, leaning down with her until he had settled her on her back in the grasses. "I have wanted you," he muttered, kissing her lips, her throat, and the upper slopes of her breasts impatiently as he began to move inside of her. "Wanted this."

She had missed it, too, so much that she felt her body begin to quake and shudder within moments. When he had found his own release, he lay panting beside her for several minutes and finally got to his feet and scooped her up, carrying her from the meadow and into the woods where she'd wakened before.

"Where are we going?" she asked lazily when he picked her up.

"Beneath the shade where the sun will not roast you, little bird," he murmured, his eyes gleaming with amusement.

She smiled back at him, burrowing her face against his shoulder, for she knew he meant to make love to her again.

It was cooler beneath the trees, darker, more intimate. He helped her from her clothing when he had set her on her feet, stoking his hands over her with both gentleness and trembling impatience, stirring her blood to feverish need once more with his urgency to explore every part of her with his lips and hands.

She lost all concept of passing time, reveling in his touch, in their joining, and the heights of passion he took her to each time they came together. Eventually, though, the world intruded. She would have been willing to ignore her body's demand for rest and sustenance only for a little time with him, but finally, reluctantly, he pulled away from her. "I must go and so must you," he murmured against her hair, stroking her soothingly as her body cooled and her heart and lungs ceased to labor.

She made a sound of complaint in her throat, but she didn't try to cling to him when he rose and left. She lay drifting lazily for a while after he'd gone, more inclined to seek sleep than food, but her stomach refused to be quieted and finally she got up and dressed to return.

Despite the aches and twinges from their vigorous appreciation of one another, she felt so completely sated and content that she was still smiling to herself when she reached the clearing around the cottage. Reality burst upon her as she paused to look around, though, realizing it must be near noon, or perhaps later.

She spied Gaelen near the pig pen, tossing slops to the sow and her piglets, which had grown by now until they were almost half the size of their mother.

A belated sense of guilt swept over her. She had abandoned her chores to seek the Hawkin, and left Gaelen to do everything by himself. She looked down at the basket in her hand. She had gathered a few things, but hardly enough to make up for her prolonged absence.

Reluctant to face him, she started across the clearing, heading for the cottage.

He intercepted her. "I will take this and clean them at the stream."

Heat was already rising into her cheeks when she looked up at him guiltily. "I did not find much," she said quickly. "It is just as well the garden is coming along."

He smiled, stroking the fingers of one hand lightly along her cheek. "Yes, a very good thing."

She stared after him blankly when he turned and left, so surprised she completely forgot that she'd been headed to the cottage to avoid a confrontation and to change before he had the chance to study her appearance too keenly.

He was humming, she realized after a moment, off key, to be sure, but still she could tell it was the tune she so often sang beneath her breath or hummed as she worked.

Feeling oddly deflated at his cheerfulness, she glanced around the yard, wondering at it for several moments, and finally hurried inside. A stew was bubbling in the cook pot. The smell sent a near painful wave of hunger through her. Rubbing her stomach, she headed to her bed chamber to clean up and rake the tangles from her hair.

To her embarrassment, she discovered as she worked the comb through her hair, that twigs and grass were tangled among the snarls. She had no looking glass, but she saw when she studied her reflection in the wash basin that her face and neck were reddened from the Hawkin's caresses, her lips swollen and her eyes almost glassy with the lingering afterglow of their coupling. She had dressed very haphazardly, as well.

How could he have failed to notice that she looked just as she was, a woman who had been thoroughly pleasured?

Puzzling over it, she dressed again when she had bathed and returned to tend the food on the hearth and set the table for their meal. Gaelen not only seemed just as cheerful when he returned, he seemed almost--enervated. "I have thought of a way to bring the water into the cottage without so much labor," he announced cheerfully as he ate.

Lilith blinked at him in surprise, but managed to assume an expression of interest as he explained that he had studied the mechanics of the miller's water wheel and thought that it would work to bring small amounts of water into a cask that could be tapped whenever they wanted water, wondering if this was the source of his enthusiasm.

It seemed odd to her, but then it occurred to her after several moments that she actually knew very little about Gaelen. He had never told her where he had come from, or what he had done before. And, truthfully, he had never seemed either particularly interested in the chores required to keep her place or handy in performing them.

She frowned when he paused, waiting, she knew, for her praise. She smiled uncomfortably. "The brook is not very wide or deep, and it does not flow very rapidly either. Do you think that would be a problem?" she asked hesitantly, because she did not want to quash his enthusiasm even though she doubted very much that it would work.

He shrugged. "A small wheel, only, and small amounts of water." He focused on his food for a few moments. "I do not at all care for the cold water for bathing, and I can not abide the stench from my labors. I am not at all certain that I can endure it when the air grows cold, as well. I know I do not desire to discover how miserable it would be."

Lilith tilted her head curiously, warmed by the fact that he seemed to assume that he would stay with her through the winter, but intrigued, too, by what he seemed to be saying about his life before. "You are not used to the cold. You are from a warmer place?"

He flicked a startled glance at her, but nodded. "Much warmer."

She was disappointed when he seemed disinclined to elaborate, but she did not press him. Instead, she withdrew into her own thoughts, trying to ignore the plaguing guilt that threaded her thoughts.

She did care for Gaelen. Whatever doubts she might have had before had certainly been put to rest when he had been hurt, for she had been devastated at the possibility of losing him. As often as not, he was morose or un-talkative, but he was still with her, giving her companionship whether he spoke or not.

It had been wrong to take the Hawkin as a lover, she thought, feeling reluctance to face it even as she made herself do so, feeling an even greater reluctance to face giving him up. She would probably not have a choice, though, she realized. She did not delude herself into believing that he would forget the woman he loved and give his love to her instead. He had needs, demands of his body that were nigh impossible to ignore. Before, she might have dismissed that, might have been more inclined to think it a lack of control than a drive. She knew better now, though. She knew what it felt like to have such a hunger eating away at her that it began to seem reasonable to take what she wanted even when she knew it wasn't at all reasonable.

It was a sort of madness, she thought abruptly, as Gaelen rose and left the cottage. He was a good man, worthy, deserving of a woman who could give him her whole heart.

Unfortunately, she did not think she could do that.

What she felt for the Hawkin was far more than lust. Desire might be the driving force of her complete disregard for every other consideration, but it was the things she had felt for him that had triggered the yearning for him in the first place.

She covered her face with her hands, so torn she could not think what to do. Only thinking about never seeing the Hawkin again was enough to make her feel as if she wanted to die, as if she *would* wither and die if he went away and she could not see him.

She felt almost the same when she tried to imagine giving up Gaelen.

Finally, she pushed the worry to the back of her mind and got up to attend the chores she had neglected, those Gaelen had not already taken care of for her. As cowardly as she knew it was, as fraught with potential disaster as she knew it was, she shied away from actually doing or saying anything herself to tip the scales. She would wait, she decided, and allow fate to decide, for *she* could not.

Chapter Thirteen

Gaelen, Lilith realized after a few days, was not merely cheerful, and excited about the idea that he had thought up. He was happy. Even when he discovered that his careful study of the Miller's wheel was not enough to make copying it easy, he kept his temper and persevered, working at it until Lilith had given up and gone inside to prepare an evening meal.

His frustration with the attempt had vanished by the time he came in to share a meal with her, and Lilith discovered why the following morning, for he had kept at it until he had the small wheel spinning as it should.

She chuckled when he gestured to it proudly. "You are so clever! But I can see that you are so pleased with yourself that you do not really need my approval," she added teasingly.

He sent her a look that was wryly amused. "I always need your approval. For I have found that I am only happy when you are."

A mixture of warmth and discomfort pricked at her. She could think of nothing to say to that, however, and tried to redirect the conversation to something less distressing. "How will you get the water from here to there?" she asked in innocent curiosity.

His amusement vanished. He frowned as he studied the distance between the brook and the cottage, which was on a rise above the brook.

Lilith bit her lip, realizing very little short of magic was going to carry the water uphill. "I am confident you will find a way," she said quickly, realizing she had inadvertently knocked the rug out from under him and beating a hasty retreat.

When she rose the following morning, Gaelen was gone. A nearly overpowering desire to slip into the forest to look for the Hawkin washed over her. She fought it. She had made up her mind that she would not go again. As much as she wanted the Hawkin, he was not for her. She had resolved to do her best to stay away from him and focus on trying to make a life with Gaelen, who seemed to have made up his mind to stay with her.

She was glad she had resisted the urge, for Gaelen showed up mid morning with a stranger. The village was small, and though she did not know many of them either by trade or name, she knew their faces well enough to know that the man must be from another village.

He was quaking, sickly pale, and sweating profusely despite the mildness of the day. She wondered if he was ill, but when she approached him to ask, he merely stared at her as if she had two heads and flatly denied it.

Abashed, Lilith retreated as the two men set about building what she finally realized was a slew to carry the water.

She smiled inwardly. Gaelen might not know how to do such things himself, but he knew how to get them done and, in the end, that was all that really mattered. He *was* clever!

She was a little surprised when the man stayed the night in the shed, but Gaelen said that was because they had not finished and the man would stay until they had worked out the matter of removing the overflow of water, and the waste.

"How much will he expect to be paid for the work?" she asked.

Gaelen looked at her blankly, searching his mind for an answer that Lilith would find acceptable, certain that she would not find it at all acceptable if he said that he had promised the man he would allow him to live if he performed the work satisfactorily. "A pig?" he hazarded.

Lilith's brows rose in surprise. "Only one? He is working very hard only for one."

"Two, then," Gaelen said irritably.

Confused by his brusque response, Lilith gaped at him, but allowed the matter to drop, wondering if it was the aggravation of the task he'd set for himself that was beginning to gnaw at the good humor that had buoyed his spirits for nigh a week, or it if was something else.

Her needs were certainly beginning to gnaw at her. Even though she had made the decision not to seek the Hawkin out again and was not happy with the necessity she felt to make that choice, she had been wrapped in a warm glow of satisfaction for days and only had to recall their time together to resurrect the happiness. After nigh a week of deprivation, however, resurrecting the memories only added to the need that had begun to tease at her again, and slowly evolved from a gentle teasing to burgeoning torment.

By the time Gaelen finished his project and went off with his worker, Lilith found she could not bear it any longer. She *had* to go. She needed the Hawkin and she could not rest or think of anything else.

She had begun to think that she had stayed away so long that the Hawkin had ceased to watch for her. She wandered the meadow for more than an hour, and finally went into the forest, calling for him in desperation, uncaring whether Gaelen returned and heard her or not.

She realized, dimly, that she was obsessed with him and the rapture he gave her, for the more she received the more she wanted. The desire for him was like a drug in her body, never completely assuaged. Instead, each time it was appeased, it built a stronger craving.

When the Hawkin at last appeared, she rushed to him with a mixture of relief, remorse, and gladness, too happy to see him to yield to the fear that had been slowly building in her as she searched for him that she would never see him again. Throwing herself into his arms, she made love to him with all of the desperation that had gathered in her while she searched for him.

It was already dark by the time she dragged herself back to the cottage and she was so exhausted from their lovemaking she could barely walk. She certainly was in no state to consider what she might tell Gaelen about her disappearance, or her bedraggled appearance when she returned for that matter.

To her surprise and relief, he did not question it. Instead, he carried her around to the back of the cottage and showed her the pool he and the worker from the distant village had made for bathing. Surrounding it was lit torches. She discovered to her surprise once he had helped her undress and get in, that the water was hot.

It felt wonderfully soothing, but despite the flicker of curiosity as to how he had managed to produce the hot water, she was too tired to care at the moment, and too grateful for it to question it.

She was a little alarmed when he stripped his own clothes off and climbed in with her, and uneasy when he began to bathe her as if she was no more than a helpless child, but his touch was soothing, unthreatening, comforting. Soothed by his attentions, weak from the heat of the water, she was more than half asleep by the time they left the pool and returned to the cottage and she was far more interested in curling up and sleeping than eating.

Gaelen was insistent, however, that she eat and when she ignored him and went to her room, he simply followed her with the food, climbing into the bed with her and teasing her by brushing tidbits across her lips until she took them. She didn't know whether to be more irritated or more amused, but she discovered that the intimacy of it warmed her far more than she was prepared to deal with at the moment.

The oddity of the entire situation had been plaguing her for a while, she realized when she went out to attend her chores the following day and discovered that Gaelen had found the ax she'd hidden from him as was very cheerfully hacking trees down to build a room for the bath. It was unnerving to watch him felling trees and Lilith retreated out of harm's way and tried to ignore his death defying attempt at construction.

He was humming again, she realized later. That did not strike her as particularly odd until she realized that she was humming happily, as well.

She had *reason* to be happy, though. She'd spent the day before with her lover.

Why in Hades was he so damned cheerful, she wondered irritably?

She dismissed the idea that first popped into her mind, that he was cheerful for the same reason she was--he had thoroughly sated himself.

It occurred to her after a while that she had been so focused on her passionate affaire, and felt so guilty after her encounters that she avoided Gaelen as much as possible, that she hadn't really been paying him a great deal of attention. Thinking back, though, she realized that his attitude had changed as radically as hers had and at around the same time.

It was almost amusing to think that both of them had found lovers and both of them were sneaking off to be with them, each struggling to hide it from the other.

Almost.

Except for the fact that the idea of Gaelen taking a lover sent a stab of jealousy through her.

It was unreasonable, she knew. She had no claim upon him, and certainly no right to make judgments when she had taken a lover. She could not help the way she felt, though, even if it was unreasonable.

And it wasn't just jealousy. It was the fear that Gaelen

would leave her for his lover and she would be alone.

Because she knew the Hawkin would not stay with her. She was actually more than a little amazed that they had been lovers as long as they had, for despite the fact that she held nothing back when she went to him, she always struggled for a very long time with her conscience before she caved in, hoping each time that she would be strong enough to ignore the siren call.

She wanted both men and she could not have both.

For the first time since she had taken the Hawkin as her lover, she found herself focusing so steadfastly on Gaelen that she began to notice things she had not noticed before, remember things that she had thought insignificant.

The thoughts that slowly began to evolve in her mind seemed so farfetched, so completely fantastic, that she dismissed it the first time it occurred to her. Once the idea had germinated, however, she could not let it go. As many times as she tried to reason it away, it kept returning.

In physical appearance, she could see that Gaelen differed as much from the Hawkin as he resembled him. The Hawkin was hairless, completely. Gaelen was hairy, with long black hair, and a beard. His chest was also hairy, his legs, his arms. She knew because he had no concern about her seeing his body and she had seen him completely naked more than once.

On the other hand, both men were of a comparable height and build and that in itself was unusual. Few mortal men were as big as Gaelen.

Both had unusual golden eyes, as well, eyes that were far too bright to be considered merely 'brown'.

They were both *called* Gaelen. As distracted as she had been she had thought that odd when she discovered it. Not amazing, because such things happened, but definitely a peculiar sort of coincidence.

It was a lot more significant that both of them called her little bird. She had thought to begin with that she was the one who was confused, but she no longer believed that. So, either the Hawkin had overheard Gaelen, which wasn't impossible, or he called her that because there was only *one* Gaelen.

The Hawkin was a demon, she reminded herself after a time. He would have powers that would seem fantastic to anyone else.

He would also have the magic to change form if he chose. She knew that much about demons. She wasn't certain why it hadn't occurred to her that that was a possibility before, but it occurred to her now.

Why would he choose to, though? That was the one question that kept coming around every time she began to be convinced that she had figured it all out. What possible reason could a demon have to trick her at all, let alone in such a way as she was considering?

She was not certain enough to want to confront either one, though. There remained just enough doubt in her mind to make her worry that she would be thought mad for even thinking up such a strange tale.

It was hard to ignore the pull to go to the Hawkin again as the days passed, but she did her best not to think about it, focusing on watching Gaelen instead. If he left, she decided, she would follow him. Then she would discover once and for all if he had a lover, or if she was right and he was the Hawkin.

She could worry about why the demon had decided to deceive her when she knew for certain that he had--*if* he had.

Gaelen did not leave, but his cheerfulness dwindled to restlessness at just about the time hers did. As miserable as she had become, she began to feel a good deal of empathy for his plight, began to think that he would not slip away because he knew she was watching him. But now that she had become certain that something very strange was going on, she meant to get to the bottom of it.

When a week had passed and she had gone from simply missing the Hawkin to a restless yearning for him, she began to think that maybe she *was* mad, maybe she had imagined there was something there that wasn't, arranging everything to suit herself rather than with any logic. There was no getting around the want she felt for both men. Had she simply invented a tale to assuage her fears, need, and guilt?

* * * *

Ordinarily, Lilith politely ignored Gaelen's difficulties with his beard and moustache at the evening meal. Like pretty much everything else, though, because of her needs it had begun to be an annoyance. She had watched him irritably dabbing at his whiskers for some moments with the napkin she had given him before her patience broke. "I should cut that off."

Gaelen paused, glanced at her in surprise, and then looked down at himself as if searching for the object that had offended. "What?" he asked uneasily.

"The whiskers," she said decisively, getting up from the table and crossing the room to her work basket where she dug around for her shears.

Gaelen had slewed around in his seat and was watching her with a mixture of wariness and irritation when she found what she was looking for and headed for him purposefully.

"Why?" he demanded.

"Because I do not like them," Lilith retorted. "I can see little of your face except for the nose and eyes, and often not much of those for the hair hanging around your face. It is like always peering at someone behind a veil. I think there is a very nice face behind all of that hair."

He stared at the shears she held up with a mixture of wariness and surprise. "I look as all the men in the village look."

"I do hope you do not mean that you prefer to look like

those unkempt louts? You should not model yourself after them. Besides, you do not seem to relish going about filthy and stinking as they do. You will be much more comfortable without it and I will be able to see you when I look at your instead of a veil of black hair."

Grasping his wrist, she gave him a tug.

He got up and allowed her to lead him to the straight chair near the hearth, but she could tell he was still uncertain of what she had in mind and not sure he wanted to cooperate. "You did not seem to mind before."

"Sit!" she said, pointing to the chair. "And I will go and fetch my comb."

He followed her into her bed chamber instead. "You did not object before," he prodded her as she grabbed the comb and headed back toward the main room of the cottage, grabbing his hand again as she pushed past him and urging him toward the chair once more.

When he sat down in the chair, she began to work the comb through his hair. "I have never been fond of a great deal of hair on a man, but I had no interest in the village louts. This is different."

He frowned. "It keeps me warm."

She glanced down at him, shook her head and chuckled. "It is not cold. I will knit something to keep you warm when the weather grows cold."

Ignoring his reluctance, she finished combing his hair and then moved around to face him to comb the tangles from the beard and moustache, wondering if his reluctance had anything to do with her seeing his face better. It had not really occurred to her before that there was a good deal of resemblance between his features--what she could see of them, and the Hawkin's. She supposed that was because she had not expected to see any similarity. In many ways, he was almost directly opposite the Hawkin, pale skinned and hairy, where the Hawkin was dark skinned and hairless.

And yet, his features were shaped much the same, she thought, his nose, his eyes, and what she could see of the line of his jaw and his lips.

When she had smoothed the hair, she took the shears and began to carefully clip the hair as closely as she could to his skin, tossing the locks she cut away into the fire. The unpleasant stench of burning hair began to sting her nose. After a moment, she left off what she was doing and moved to the door to open it and the shutters on the windows to allow the evening air to circulate through the cottage.

She leaned close to him as she worked, so focused on her task and making certain she cut closely without nicking his skin that it was several moments before she noticed that his gaze was riveted to her bodice. She also noticed a faint tremor in him as she stroked her hands over his face.

"Are you chilled?"

He cleared his throat. "Nay," he said finally.

Smiling inwardly, she straightened to view her handiwork as she finished trimming the beard and tossed the last of the hair onto the hearth. "Better," she announced somewhat breathlessly, feeling her own body warm from her proximity to him. She hesitated for several moments and finally lifted her skirts and settled astride his lap, shifting closer to clip the hair from his upper lip. His eyes widened in momentary surprise at her boldness, but then narrowed, gleaming heatedly. His hands settled lightly on her waist.

Dragging in a deep breath, Lilith focused on keeping her hands steady as she carefully trimmed the excess hair from his upper lip. Finally, seeing that she had cut as closely as she could with the shears without risking nicking his skin, she dropped the comb and shears beside the chair and brushed his face and the front of his shirt to remove the hair she'd cut.

"Goodness," she exclaimed, forcing a faint smile as she studied his face. "I had no notion you were so handsome." As handsome as the Hawkin.

He looked pleased. "I am pleasing to your eyes?"

She smiled with less effort at his blatant demand for more praise. "You have always been pleasing to my eyes, Gaelen," she murmured, looping her arms around his neck and leaning close to brush her lips along his.

His hands tightened on her waist for a fraction of a second and then he wrapped his arms tightly around her, opening his mouth over hers. What little doubt remained that her mind was playing tricks on her vanished. She knew him.

He might change his appearance, but his taste and his touch, the way he kissed her and held her were unmistakable. A fiery tide of welcome broke through her restraint, washing the last of her doubts from her mind and with it any thoughts of demanding answers to the questions that descended upon her. The only thing that mattered at the moment was his touch, the delicious sensations that erupted inside of her with lightning swiftness.

She broke the kiss after a moment, dizzy with need, nuzzling her face against his, exploring his cheek to his ear, trembling as he trembled with barely leashed passion. "Make love to me, Gaelen," she murmured against his ear, nipping at the lobe with her lips as she rocked back and forth along the hard ridge of flesh between her thighs.

He dropped his hands to her waist, pushing her back along his thighs and fumbled with his breeches. In a moment, she felt his heated flesh against her belly, felt him urging her with his hands to lift up to sheathe him.

Eager to feel him deeply within her, she rose up until he could fit their bodies together and settled again, allowing the weight of her body and his hands to force her body over his turgid flesh. By the time they had managed a deep connection, she was already quivering on the brink of crisis, gasping hoarsely, almost sobbing with the fiery need coursing through her body.

He arched his hips upward, burrowing deeper still, holding himself tightly inside of her for many moments until his restraint broke and he began to urge her to move, lifting her slightly and then allowing her to slide down his shaft again and again, rocking his hips each time to meet her. Goose flesh broke along her skin as she moved, struggling to find the rhythm that would send her over the edge, crying out when she found it and ecstasy thundered through her. He uttered a throaty groan as her body began to convulse around him, milking him of his seed. His arms tightened almost crushingly around her as he found his own surcease.

Shuddering, he held her tightly, his face against the side of her neck as he gasped hoarsely to catch his breath. Abruptly, he rose straight up. Surprised, Lilith gasped, instinctively wrapping her legs around his waist and tightening her grip on his neck.

Without a word, he carried her into her bedchamber, sprawling across her bed with her and kissing her lips, her face, her throat, murmuring her name in a lover's litany of appreciation.

Shedding his clothing, he began to remove hers item by item, kissing each part of her bare skin he exposed, until, by the time they were both naked, they were caught up again in heated passion, coupling with wild abandon.

* * * *

Lilith wasn't certain whether it was the sound of labor outside the cottage that woke her or the thin mote of light weakly piercing her shutters, but she roused to a sense of intense satisfaction and well being.

Stretching, she lay staring up at her ceiling for a time, listening, recalling her night with Gaelen.

After a time the warmth began to fade and doubt crept into her mind.

She knew now that there was only one Gaelen, *her* Gaelen. She just didn't know why he had gone to such lengths to deceive her.

She puzzled over it for a while, but although random

possibilities presented themselves, she realized she would not find answers in her own mind. She might not find answers if she confronted Gaelen, but she would certainly come closer to doing so than merely speculating.

He was of the demon breed, she reminded herself. Perhaps he needed no motive at all? Perhaps he had only been amusing himself?

She could not say that she knew a great deal about them. No one did as far as she knew, though they were not slow to make up tales, for all that. But one thing everyone seemed to agree on was that demons were prone to deceiving mortals for their own ends.

She needed to know why, she realized. If she knew, then perhaps she would know if he meant to stay, or if he was only amusing himself with her.

Getting up finally, she bathed in the water in her wash basin and dressed.

Gaelen was working on the room he had decided to add to the cottage to enclose the bathing pool he had made. Smiling at him when he glanced her way, she went to the shed and got feed for the small flock of geese she and Gaelen had appropriated from the wild. The hatchlings were half grown now. The mother goose still looked at her with malice whenever she went into the pen, but the young geese had no such reservations about her. The moment she went into the pen they gathered to squabble over the feed.

Soon, they would be old enough to begin to lay and she would have eggs, she thought a little absently, making a mental note to gather the makings of nests.

When she had fed them, she went to check the progress of her garden, pulling the weeds that grew around the plants and then selecting a mess of maturing greens for her cook pot.

Gaelen moved up behind her as she settled to wash the greens, wrapping his arms around her waist and nuzzling his face against her neck. She paused, lifting a hand to caress his cheek. "You will have no food to fill your belly when you are hungry if you keep this up," she murmured.

He chuckled. "I am more interested in filling yours."

She laughed, but shook her head. "Now. Later, when you are hungry the story will be different."

He sucked a love bite along the side of her neck and released her. "Go then. I have learned patience."

Smiling to herself, she gathered the food and went in to the cottage to put it on to cook. He did have patience, she thought, looking back over the time they had spent together, infinite patience. How like a demon was that, she wondered? Patience, gentleness, kindness--at least to her. She could not recall that he had ever behaved as she would have expected a demon to behave--unless, perhaps, she counted his carnal appetite, and she could not say that hers was any less avid than his.

She realized as she was cleaning up after their noon meal that she had spent the entire morning avoiding what she knew she had to do. The temptation was strong to simply bury her head and hide from the truth, and hide from her fear that one day she would awake to find herself alone.

She would not hurt any more tomorrow or the next day if she discovered that he had only decided to amuse himself with her for a time.

She would not hurt less if she discovered it today.

She still had to know.

Taking her basket, she left the cottage and followed the path into the woods. She did not look back to see if Gaelen followed her. She knew he would. He would know that she was heading toward their rendezvous in the forest.

She discovered that she was right. When she reached the grassy clearing beneath the trees where they had lain together so many times before, he dropped from the boughs overhead, landing a short distance from her.

Instead of going to him at once as she usually did, she studied him, feeling her belly clench with desire, but also dread. She skated a hand down her belly over the roundness that had become more and more noticeable with time. Swallowing with an effort, she met his gaze. "This child is yours."

Several emotions chased across his face; relief, remorse, wariness, anxiety. His throat worked. "Yes," he said finally.

"It was my memory you took."

His face contorted, this time with pain. "Yes."

Her heart seemed to twist in her chest. She moved toward him slowly and put her arms around his waist, holding herself tightly to him. A jolt went through him, as if of surprise and then, cautiously, he wrapped his arms around her.

"Why?" she asked in a muffled voice. "Why would you do that? Why would you take my memories?"

She heard him swallow and pulled away to look up at him.

"You asked," he said hoarsely. "I promised."

A pang of loss went through her, of dread as it teased her mind to wonder why she would have demanded such a thing--and yet he had said that he loved her. She had seen in the way he looked at her. She frowned. "Give them back."

He looked a little ill. He lifted a hand to her cheek, cupping it. "I can not, little bird. That is why I did not want to take them, because I could not give them back and I knew that all that had happened, all that had been between us would be lost to you. It has been the worst sort of torture to me to remember and to know that you do not."

She studied his face, trying to fathom the anxiety she saw behind his regret. "Were any of the things you told me true?" she asked finally, pulling away from him.

The wariness returned to his eyes. "Which things?" he asked cautiously.

She gave him a look. "I know you are the man who lives

with me," she said flatly. "You deceived me. Why?"

Anger flickered in his eyes, and doubt. "I did not set out to deceive you."

"It is just as well, for if I had not been so distracted, I would not have been deceived at all!" she said tartly.

His lips tightened. "I would have completely deceived you and you would never have guessed the truth if I had set out to do so."

"Why do it at all?"

He studied her anxiously for a moment and finally sat down, drawing his knees up and dropping one elbow to his knee. Cupping his chin in his hand, he glared at nothing in particular. "I only wanted to know if you would find me more pleasing if you believed I was a man," he said shortly. "When I saw that you did, then I could not resist staying, but I had not set out to deceive you and I did not know how to behave as a mortal man. If I had planned to deceive you, then I would have learned the things I needed to know before I went to you."

She stared down at him irritably for a moment, and finally knelt down, pushed his arms aside and climbed onto his lap, settling his arms around her waist and leaning her head against his shoulder. Surprised, he simply allowed her to arrange herself as she pleased. "That was a great deal of trouble to go to," she murmured, "only to appease your curiosity."

"I was not curious!" he said. "I was … desperate. You are not angry with me again? I will *not* take your memory again. I have endured as much of this as I can bear. I do not want to have to try again."

She sent him a look, amused and touched by his unwitting assertion that he *would* try again. "I was before?"

"I do not wish to discuss that," he said tightly. "You do not remember because you did not want to remember, and you are mine now, so it does not matter."

A mixture of irritation and amusement filled her. "And

how do you know that?" she demanded.

He caught her jaw in one large hand. "You gave yourself to me, as the man, Gaelen, and as I am. I did not take. You gave. You said that you cared for me."

She met his gaze unflinchingly. "Did you give yourself to me?"

He frowned. "Yes."

"You do not sound certain. Did you not mean it, then, when you said you loved the mortal woman?"

He seemed to war with himself a moment. "I did not say I loved the mortal woman. *You* said that I loved her. I only said that I was ... that I could not bear to let her go. That I had to find a way to make her love me."

She smiled. "Why would that matter, whether she loved you or not, if you did not love her?"

He dragged in a shaky breath. "I do not know. I am Hawkin. I can not say that I understand the strange ways of mortals. And you know very well that there is no 'she'," he retorted irritably. "You know that I meant you."

"This entire charade was to woo me then?" she asked, pleased. "Because you love me? And you mean to stay with me?"

He looked conflicted. Finally, he smiled wryly. His arms tightened around her, squeezing her just enough to reassure her. "You have a fearsome temper, little bird. But I am Hawkin, and fearless. I will brave your wrath if I must, and I will return even if you send me away again, always, forever. If that is love, then yes, I love you--more each day than the day before."

The End

Don't miss out on collecting these other exciting Harmony™ titles for your collection:

The Devil's Concubine by Jaide Fox (Fantasy Romance) Trade Paper 1-58608-776-2
A great contest was announced to decide who would win the hand of Princess Aliya, accounted the fairest young maiden in the land. The ruler of every kingdom was invited--every kingdom that is save those of the unnaturals. When King Talin, ruler of the tribe of Golden Falcons learned of the slight, he was enraged. He had no desire to take a mere man child as his bride, but he would allow the insult to go unchallenged.

Zhang Dynasty: Seduction of the Phoenix by Michelle M. Pillow (Futuristic Romance) Trade Paper 1-58608-777-0
A prince raised in honor and tradition, a woman raised with nothing at all. She wants to steal their most sacred treasure. He'll do anything to protect it, even if it means marrying a thief.

Warriors of the Darkness by Mandy M. Roth (Paranormal Romance) Trade Paper 1-58608-778-9
In place where time and space have no boundaries, ancient enemies would like nothing more than to eradicate them both, just when they've found each other.

Clone Wars: Armageddon by Kaitlyn O'Connor (Futuristic Romance) Trade Paper 1-58608-775-4
Living in a world devastated by one disaster after another, it's natural for people to look for a target to blame for their woes, and Lena thinks little of it when new rumors begin to circulate about a government conspiracy. She soon discovers, though, that the government may or may not be conspiring against its citizens, but someone certainly is. Morris, her adoptive father, isn't Morris anymore, and the mirror image of herself that comes to kill her most definitely isn't a long lost identical twin.

Printed in the United States
53001LVS00004B/1-150